No Longer Warriors

Charles H. Harrison

PublishAmerica

Baltimore

First printing

ISBN: 1-59129-981-0 (softcover)
ISBN: 978-1-4489-1054-0 (hardcover)
PUBLISHED BY PUBLISHAMERICA BOOK PUBLISHERS
www.publishamerica.com
Baltimore

Printed in the United States of America

Dedication

For Cindy, who first went with me to reconnoiter, down a lane and in the rain, the house on the Gettysburg battlefield that became the focal point of this novel, and for Charlotte Ann, who read the first draft and smiled a smile that told me this story of six wounded and scarred soldiers confined as strangers in that house was worth the telling.

I love them both.

"The history of a soldier's wound beguiles the pain of it."
Laurence Sterne ~ *Tristram Shandy, Book I*

PROLOGUE

In the late afternoon of July 2, 1863, Corporal Noah B. Kimbark of Company H, 124th New York Volunteer Regiment—the Orange Blossoms (because they came from Orange County)—was shot through the breast while defending Devils' Den at Gettysburg from attack by the First Texas Regiment.

Kimbark was an uncle of David and John Kidd, also members of the 124th. David was my great-grandfather.

What happened to Kimbark in the minutes, hours and days after he was wounded is recorded in the regimental history:

"I was unconscious for a short time. When I recovered my senses, the Rebels were advancing over me. I remained where I fell until the next morning, when one of their officers came along and ordered me to go to the rear. I managed to crawl a rod or so alone. Then he sent a man to assist me. But the fellow said I would die anyway and soon left me.

"Then I crawled to a fence and lay down again by it. There was a Rebel picket post near me and one of the men came and gave me a swallow of water from his canteen. Presently another one of them came along with a four gallon earthen jug on his head which he had just filled at some spring, and stopped and gave me a good drink, after which I fell asleep.

"When I awoke, their pickets had gone; but before long, a Rebel battle line advanced past me and their officers ordered me to crawl further to the rear. Presently a burial party with picks and shovels came along and I asked them where their hospital was. They said it was a short distance beyond in a piece of woods—that some of them were going there presently after water, and would take me with them, which they did.

"It was not a regular hospital—only a sort of stopping place for the wounded. A Rebel doctor who was there came to see me and inquired where I was wounded. And when I told him I was shot through the lungs, he replied, 'Oh, that will not kill you,' gave me some morphine on the blade of a pocket knife and said there would soon be an ambulance there to take me to the hospital.

"Just then, shells from our batteries began to fall among us and their ambulance teams were driven up on a run, and the stretcher bearers rushed in among us and carried off all the Rebel wounded but left me sitting there alone, leaning against a tree.

"There was a small log barn close by and I crept into it. There were two Rebels in there. One of them was very badly wounded and the other one (not wounded) was taking care of him. They did not speak to me, and I lay down on some straw and soon fell asleep. When I awoke, there was an ambulance at the door taking in the wounded Rebel. I asked them to take me too, but they did not let on that they heard me and drove off, and I was alone again.

"Presently I saw some Confederates pass by carrying a wounded officer and I got on my feet and tried to follow them, for I thought they must be going to some hospital. I managed to get several rods, then my strength failed me and I had to sink down, and they were soon out of sight.

"But there was a small stream close by and some men who came to get water told me there was a house a short distance ahead with a lot of wounded 'Yanks' in it. After a while I got to this house and remained there two nights."

This novel was inspired by Kimbark's ordeal.

8

CHAPTER ONE
Corporal Seth Adams

Seth Adams lay on his back, an Orange Blossom beginning to wilt under a bright sun only partly obscured by a leaden scum of humidity and smoke and a sweeping black cloud of turkey vultures that banked right and then left, eyes bulging from their lumpy red head that the Maker of All Creatures must first have discarded as too ugly and ill-formed to attach to any body. Only later did the Maker retrieve the damned thing from the trash and plunk it upon that dark stump, hardly a neck to speak of. This morning those vulture eyes spotted dead and dying flesh as far as they could see, some swollen carrion wrapped in blue, some in gray.

Colonel A. Van Horne Ellis, commander of the 124th New York Volunteers from Orange County, had first invoked the nickname Orange Blossoms at the battle of Chancellorsville in May. "Hi, hi my Orange Blossoms," he said as he ordered the regiment to fix bayonets and dislodge the foe from Union works they had recently captured. Ellis's orders always were heard and obeyed, but he didn't bellow or exhort like so many other colonels. He sat straight on his horse, arms folded as though he were watching his troops run through the manual of arms on the parade ground instead of seeing them killing and being killed on bloody ground. From the first time he had looked up at Ellis high in the saddle when the regiment assembled in Goshen last summer, Seth thought Ellis's eyes didn't belong to a warrior. There was a softness and a kind of melancholy in them that better suited a poet or artist.

After Chancellorsville, where forty percent of the regiment had fallen down dead or wounded, the Orange Blossoms, along with the rest of the Army of the Potomac, sulked and waited for the Army of Northern Virginia to blink first — to reveal its next intention. Lee's rebels finally moved out in June, crossed the Potomac and headed north behind the Blue Ridge. The Union army, now under George Meade, roughly paralleled the rebel line of march, but was strung out along several Maryland roads that, in the summer heat, sent up great swirls of dust to sting the eyes and clog the noses of the plodding soldiers. The Orange Blossoms had encamped at Emmitsburg just below the Pennsylvania border, where they gorged on cherries from nearby orchards and deposited the pits in their shit trenches. July 1 commenced a lazy day. Some men snoozed in the shade of an old hickory, others played faro or poker, and not a few scribbled notes to family. Near two o'clock in the afternoon, the unmistakable sound of distant artillery fire rolled down from somewhere up north, bounced off the Blue Ridge and rolled over the camp like an ominous thunder the foot soldier knew as the portent of deadly lightning — the flash of musket and cannon. The bugles blew, the orders shouted, and the Orange Blossoms formed up with other regiments and divisions, and together they quick timed toward the noise of battle. By the time they arrived, two miles south of Gettysburg according to an officer who unfolded a crude map of the area, the fighting had subsided, and they were safe from that terrible lightning for one day longer.

Yesterday, Colonel Ellis led the regiment to its assigned position on a ridge at the rear of and above the massive remains of a glacial upheaval the locals called Devil's Den. To their left was James Smith's battery of four ten-pounder Parrots, and on their right in the woods was the New York Eighty-sixth. In front of the Orange Blossoms was a boulder-strewn three acres of open ground shaped like an equilateral triangle. The 124th was positioned at one point, with the base of the triangle at the bottom of a long slope that ran into a stone wall. On the other side of the stone wall was Plum Run, a decent brook in a heavy rain storm, but mostly a muddy trickle at this time of year. Looking beyond Plum

Run the Orange Blossoms from their perch could see through second or third growth trees how the terrain sloped up again toward a distant ridge upon which sat on its haunches ready to spring John B. Hood's conglomeration of wiry Texans, Georgians and Alabamians.

At about half past four, when the sun was perhaps three field glass levels above the distant mountains to the west, the Confederate tide went forward in waves, down off the far ridge and into Plum Run valley. No yell, yet, from the throats of that motley crowd — that terrible wailing that sounded two decibels above an eagle's screech. The gray line, several ranks deep, climbed easily over the low stone wall at the bottom of the triangle and halted. Out front was the First Texas, men and boys from the far reaches of the Confederacy, likely not one a slaveholder. They cast their eyes 300 feet up the slope and met the glare of 220 farmers and sundry craftsmen and handymen from such places as Newburgh, New Windsor and Wallkill. Then the Texans caterwauled and rushed forward. Seth, standing three men from the flag bearer, leveled his musket and as one the front rank fired into the advancing Texans, many of whom fell like young pines lining the Red River. They regrouped — they always did — and again pushed onward and upward, the rebel yell now buried in their gut after the first terrible shock of battle.

As Seth remembered it, at about the time the Texans came at the Orange Blossoms again, Major James Cromwell, a reckless and fearless warrior, mounted his horse, waved his sword frantically above his head and then brought it down in the direction of the rebels. The 124th rushed down the triangular field, cracking the wall of Texans and sending most of them running and stumbling back down the hill. But officers on horseback become easy targets that even the newest recruit can hit, and Cromwell took a minie ball to the heart and fell backward off his horse. With his death, the charge of the Orange Blossoms commenced falling apart. Besides, the Texans were reinforced by a fresh Georgia regiment, and the 124th pulled back to regain — temporarily as it turned out — the crest of the ridge above Devil's Den, the point of the triangle.

As Seth turned to follow the regiment back up the slope, two things happened almost simultaneously. First, he glimpsed Ellis through the gritty smoke rise up in his stirrups and point his sword straight toward the blue sky no one on the ground could see any longer. Again a target, and again a deeply tanned and scrawny Texan, who himself might be killed at any moment took aim, fired and hit his mark. The man of the sad eyes, who had promised when the 124th received its regimental banner and national flag, "If you never again see these colors, you will never again see those who bear them from you," fell forward among the boulders. Almost at that precise moment, Seth felt a sharp pain halfway down his back that traveled through his chest cavity and came out somewhere to the right of where he supposed his heart and lungs to be. The pain was not great at first, but as he tried to continue running it ached to breathe deeply, and his feet and legs felt as though he were slogging through swamp. Then he was no longer running, and it grew dark inside his head; explosions, screams and moans faded until he no longer heard them at all.

When he regained consciousness during the night — he had no idea what time it was — Seth was in a fetus position, and his chest hurt nearly as badly as a woman's belly about to expel a stillborn child. At first, he could detect no sound, as though he were alone on this piece of earth where only hours ago thousands of men tried desperately and noisily to slaughter one another. Then his ears picked up a scattering of sounds, some far away and others nearby, but all muted as if no one dared risk raising the dead or inviting a bullet from one side or another. A canteen clinked as someone fetched it or slung it back over a tent pole, sticks crackled and little stones crunched as a sentry or picket changed positions, and a pet dog barked twice. From quite distant — Seth had no idea where the opposing lines were by now — a solo tenor softly sang, "Sweet hour of prayer that calls me from a world of care and bids me at my father's throne make all my wants and wishes known." Wants and wishes, indeed, Seth thought. I don't want to die at age 25, and I wish to hell I was sleeping in my bed at home in Walden.

Home. Dearest Goose. In his letters, that's how he greeted his fiancee, Lorannah Vandergost, and she wrote back, Dearest Yank. They corresponded frequently, but since the army's been on the move, for reasons no one could explain convincingly, mail had not been reaching

12

the army, or at least not the 124th New York. Lately, perhaps because of the absence of letters, Seth had taken to imagining what Goose might report about life at home or what she might say to him at any given moment or in some circumstance. He thought he heard her warn him about eating the cherries in Maryland: "Hey, Yank, those things are going to give you the runs real bad." She was right, of course.

And he talked in his mind to her:

Dearest Goose, I've been shot, and I don't know how bad it is. I hurt like the devil, but I don't think — oh, God, don't let me die here, not alone, not far from the ones I love and who love me. I think of you often and miss you always. Goddamn war — excuse me Goose. Say hello to my folks. Do you here me, Goose? Am I getting through?

At one point during the long and dreadful night, Seth turned over on his back and stretched out his arm until his hand felt something soft that squished at his touch. When he brought back his hand, he saw in the faint light of the moon what appeared to be a smear of blood and brain on his thumb and forefinger. Once he was roused by someone tripping over him and falling heavily to the ground.

"Who are you?" Seth asked softly.

"Posey McBride," was the weak response.

"What unit?"

"Twentieth Georgia. And you?" His voice was almost a whisper and raspy.

"One hundred twenty-fourth New York."

"Say, yank, got any water?"

"None."

"Oh well, guess it wouldn't do no good anyway."

"Why's that?"

"Cause I'm already dead. Got a hole in my gut bigger than my fist and it's gettin' harder to push my intestines back in. They keep slidin' out and dribbling down my pants leg. Damndest thing, you know. Where are you hit?"

"In the chest. Hurts bad when I breathe."

"Hell, yank, you're liable to croak ahead of me." There was a long silence. "No, I reckon not." The voice was barely audible and strained. "I'm on my way to the promised land. Here I come, God, ready or not." He lay down next to Seth and folded his arms over his chest as though he had been laid out by an undertaker.

Seth heard Posey McBride's life's breath rattle away on that Pennsylvania field of ancient stones and recently scythed grass now matted in gore hundreds of miles from the red clay of Georgia and a way of life that had always seemed to Seth to be light years away from how they lived in Orange County, New York.

Just before dawn, when the sun was fighting the moon for dominance in the sooty sky, he had seen Stretch Martin of Company H walking toward him through the mist. Well, he wasn't walking exactly, more like a drunk reeling after an all-night toot. Stretch was perhaps ten feet away when Seth noticed the blood-soaked rag around his head and the crimson tide that flowed slowly down his forehead and into his eyes.

"Stretch, for God's sake!"

"That you, Seth?" Stretch squinted through his bloody eyes.

"Yes. Where do you think you're going?"

"Well, I rightly guess I'm going to see Lucy and the children. Are you comin'?"

"I don't think so, Stretch. How are you going to get there? It's a long way, you know."

"Oh, I'll make it. I figger I'm almost home when I reach the Wallkill River. And you know me, Seth, I can smell water from afar off, even in summer when the level of the river is down to nothin' more than a thirsty creek. And by God, Seth, I smell water ahead. If you're not comin' with me, I'll just have to see you when you do get home. Bye." Seth raised up off the ground on an elbow and watched as Stretch staggered down the slope. He was almost out of sight when he stopped, stood straight as a stately New York oak tree, and then pitched forward as though he had been cut down in the forest.

And now the sun was up, and it was July 3. Suddenly, the sun's rays were completely blocked by a large round head topped with a Confederate officer's tattered hat. Seth couldn't see the lips move under the rusty beard splotched by battle grime, but the words were plain enough. "Yank, move your ass to the rear. You're getting in the way of my men."

"I'm not sure that I can, sir. My chest is full of hot coals fighting to get out. A bullet passed through my chest; at least I think it came out. Perhaps if you could…"

"No time, yank. Besides, you can look for help in the rear. Someone will take a look at you I'm sure. I just don't want you here. Things could get busy before long. We could be moving cannon and…well…git!" Just as suddenly, the sun flashed back into Seth's eyes.

Easy for him to order me rearward, Seth thought. *He doesn't have to crawl on his hands and knees with his lungs on fire and wheezing air like a bagpipe. And where am I supposed to go? I don't have the faintest idea what's ahead of me, what I might find behind their lines. Shit, I don't even know which direction to go in. Besides, I have to get my head together before I try moving this hurting body.*

"Hey you, yank, I told you to git, and I'm not in the habit of repeating orders."

Seth, in his daze, looked around but could not locate the voice. However, he started to crawl down the hill, away from the scene of the Orange Blossoms' gallant but fruitless charge. Out of the corner of his right eye he saw a long row of bodies lying side by side. Were they men of the 124th or were they Texans or Georgians? His head drooped. They were Orange Blossoms all right. He could tell because the rebel sons of bitches had stripped the bodies of shoes and trousers and left them in their underwear to bloat and stink under the summer sun.

"Hey, yank, you ain't goin' far crawling like some goddamned animal." Seth looked up into the face of a young man with acned face, bloodshot eyes and hair standing up and out and every which way. He was attired in the usual reb uniform of indeterminate origin—some Confederate issue, a little homespun with a piece or two of Federal blue.

"Do you think I like this position, reb, and with a hole in my chest, to boot?"

15

"I reckon not. Anyways, the captain sent me over to help you off the field."

"So help, dammit."

The johnnie bent down, grabbed Seth in the armpits and lifted him in one motion to his wobbly feet. "Thar, now, see iffen you can walk. I'll guide you."

To begin with, Seth was woozy from being yanked to a standing position before his head could adjust to the height. Furthermore, his legs were rubber, so he sagged and tilted and mostly fell against the young rebel.

"You're in pretty bad shape, yank. Iffen you're right about the hole in your chest, you're probably half dead anyways. I reckon maybe we're both wastin' our time trying to get you to someplace you ain't goin' to get to anyhow." He started to walk away, leaving Seth teetering, then turned to look back. "Say, dyin' ain't so bad. I was chargin' with a buddy yesterday and he liked to fall flat on his face. I thought he'd been hit, but when I bent down, he said his heart had gived out and…"— the reb snapped his finger— "…he was gone." The man disappeared and Seth sank once more to his hands and knees.

He reached a stone wall and collapsed. He was sucking air like a man in water over his head about to go under for the third and last time. His knees were sore and bruised; the palms of his hands and the tips of his fingers were scraped and bleeding from clawing stubble and rocks. He leaned against the stone wall facing up the hill he had just come down.

Now, he could visualize yesterday's battle through the eyes of the Texans and the Georgians who swarmed after them. The Texans' first wave had formed behind this very wall. He and his comrades on the crest had seen them massing, bayonets flashing in the late afternoon sun. They had clambered over the wall, reformed, cranked up that infernal reb screeching and started up the hill at a trot. Seth imagined that long line suddenly running into the first volley fired by him and his comrades on the crest above Devil's Den and the shells from Smith's battery to the left of the Orange Blossoms.

Seth wiped the sweat off his face with a sleeve. *Texas,* he wondered, *where exactly is that?* He knew Virginia by now and he had a pretty good notion that the Carolinas and Georgia lay somewhere south of Virginia. But Texas? That must be a really long way from here. He tried to recall the map of the United States hanging on the wall of the cold, damp schoolroom ruled by the cold, hard Miss Thorpe. Texas was almost in Mexico, for crying out loud! Those rebs who had scrambled over this wall were practically foreigners. Seth suspected some of them were Indians — heathens with red skin, black hair and black eyes who killed white people for sport. Or so he had read once.

Seth closed his eyes, attempting to drive out his pain by creating mental images of Indians. He had seen only a black and white drawing of Indians in a book, so now he relied on remembered fragments of descriptions in the book. He even managed to chill himself in the morning's heat by conjuring up fearsome faces painted in vivid colors with eyes that drilled into his and…

"Water, yank?" Seth opened his eyes to see a reb squatting in front of him holding a canteen. "Just one swallow now. Ain't all that much water left in this here canteen, and it may be all I get for a while."

Seth filled his mouth. Before the water had reached his gullet, the canteen was pulled away. "Thanks, reb." The soldier left as quietly and quickly as he had come.

The swallow had not quenched Seth's thirst, but had served to remind him how terribly parched he was—and hungry. His last meal had been lunch yesterday, such as it was. A scant ration of hardtack, with the morning's cold coffee to soften it enough so it could be chewed without breaking one's teeth.

Seth decided he would attempt getting over the wall, an obstacle he normally would have scaled with ease. Be he wasn't feeling normal, and he actually had to plan his movements. He calculated he would crawl along until he found where the wall was at its lowest and narrowest; then, he would raise himself up by holding on to the rocks, and finally tumble over, protecting his head and face as best he could. The wall was roughly three feet high where he was.

He had gone perhaps twenty feet to his left when he reached a corner where the wall turned to go back up the hill. For whatever reason—

perhaps a cannonball had struck it—the wall at this point had crumbled and the stones scattered. He got to the other side by awkward movements using his hands and feet only, never touching the rocks with his knees or any other part of his body.

However, the exertion again resulted in labored breathing and a terrible ache in his chest. He propped himself up against a small tree and surveyed the terrain in front of him. Since the sun was behind him—he guessed the time to be around eight o'clock— he must be facing west or southwest. The ground continued to slope downward for another hundred feet or so, it appeared, into a narrow valley, and then slanted up, rather sharply in places, through more boulders and trees to an elevation Seth figured might be about the same or perhaps greater than the crest where the Orange Blossoms had been positioned above the place called Devil's Den. He could see reb pickets off to his left.

He heard a noise to his right and saw a reb walking along the wall carrying a large earthen jug. Seth assumed he was heading for the pickets. The man stopped in front of him.

"This here jug is filled with water, yank. I wished it were the whiskey my old man makes, and I wished it weren't so cloudy, but it's cold and wet and I be offering you some."

"Bless you." This time it was not just a swallow. The reb let Seth drink until he motioned the jug away. "I'm mighty grateful, reb. You've probably saved my life."

"Well, I guess that's okay, unless you get back on your feet and come after us agin. In that case, I would say to myself, 'Hiram, you good-natured son-of-a-bitch, why did you give that wounded yankee a drink so's he could get well and take to shootin' some more at you and your friends.' Well, I'm off. Keep livin' yank, but no more fightin'. Promise?"

"Yes, and thanks."

For that long drink of water, Seth would have promised to shoe Jeff Davis' horse. But if he recovered from his wound sufficiently to go back on active duty, and if he were to once again face Hiram's unit in battle, he would have to refrain from shooting. That was the least he could do.

For every increase in the degree of angle formed by the sun's position relative to the earth, the heat went up two degrees. Or so it seemed. The heat and the effort expended in crawling, combined to put Seth to sleep propped against the tree.

His slumber was short-lived. He awakened to the noise of a rebel line advancing from the valley in front of him. They didn't appear to be heading into battle, but he guessed they might be preparing for a Union attack or, just as likely, relieving troops who had occupied Devil's Den since yesterday evening. "We're goin' to whop your friends again today," exulted one man as he passed by. Another shouted, "You're lucky to be wounded, yank, because we aim to kill plenty of blue bellies today." The arrogant bastards, Seth thought, but gave no reply.

"You better get outta here," said an officer. "You're in our way. Move to the rear."

They keep telling me to move to the rear, Seth thought, but where the hell is that? What is the rear? He could see the big round top up ahead, but he had no idea which army commanded it. He decided to keep moving in that direction anyway, approximately southwest.

Now, I'll show these rebs. I'm not finished yet, Seth told himself, and with difficulty he stood up almost straight and started to plod to his left. He hadn't gone far, however, when he felt weak and dropped again to all fours. *That reb was right,* he admitted. *I do crawl like the wounded animal I am.*

In this position, most of what he saw was the ground under him and a few feet ahead. Every fifteen or twenty feet, however, he stopped to look up, and on the second occasion of checking out his surroundings he saw a rebel burial party carrying picks and shovels and coming from his right rear.

"Where are you men heading?"

"To the hospital yonder." A man motioned forward. "Why?"

"Would you take me? I could sure use a doctor."

"Could you now? What do you say boys? Should we take this yankee with us or leave him to face his fate here?" The other two men grunted. "They've agreed to help you to the hospital. You ought to feel mighty grateful. Usually those boys shoot anything blue that moves. But they're on burial detail this morning and not feelin' too frisky. Plus, they don't have their muskets. Can you stand, yank?"

"I think so, but if you could help…"

The speaker and one of the other soldiers assisted Seth to his feet and allowed him to lean on them. They walked him slowly until they came to a clearing where half a dozen or more wounded rebels were lying on the ground in a rough semicircle.

One soldier's right foot was purple and black pulp where most of his toes used to be. Another man's head was almost completely swathed in bandage. The wounds of the remaining rebs were not apparent. The doctor—he was wearing a long coat that was once white—bent over a soldier whose face was flushed. Heat stroke, Seth guessed. The men who were helping Seth let him down on the ground where he sat cross-legged.

"The doc'll take care of you, yank. We're going to get ourselves a drink and then go back to the grislies."

"The what?"

"The grislies. Buryin' friend and foe. We've been at it since before dawn. We had to reopen one grave when we found the man's head ten feet away."

The burial party got their drinks from one of two large earthen jars sitting on a nearby stump and then clomped off to the east. Seth was afraid he'd roll over from his unsteady sitting position, so he crawled to a tree and leaned against it. He looked up and noticed that most of its branches had been blown away by cannon fire.

For ten or fifteen minutes, the doctor paid no attention to Seth; he seemed almost to purposely ignore him. When he finally came over, he squatted down on his haunches in front of Seth.

"You look all right, son. What's the problem?"

"I was shot through the lungs. I mean a bullet must have passed through my chest. It hurts to breathe and I don't seem to have much energy."

"Did you lose much blood?"

"I don't think so."

"Here, turn around so I can see your back." Seth moved away from the tree to allow the doctor to pull up his jacket and shirt and examine his back. "A clean hole and very little external bleeding. Of course, it's hard to know what's going on inside, but I believe you'll live."

"I think the bullet came out here." Seth again raised his shirt and jacket and motioned toward his right side below the nipple. "I've poked around a little and I'm pretty sure I felt something."

The doctor examined the spot. "You're right. That's where the bullet emerged. It's a bit of a jagged wound, but again there doesn't seem to have been much bleeding. I'm going to give you a little morphine—and a little is all I got left—to ease your pain." He opened the kit he had brought with him, stuck in his pocket knife, and came out with some powder on the blade. "Here, lick this off." Seth did as he was told. "Now, lean back against the tree. I expect an ambulance or two soon that will take these men to a real hospital. We can probably get you in, too."

It couldn't have been more than five minutes when two ambulances—nothing more than flat-bottomed boxes on wheels—came at a slow trot down the valley from the north. They had just come to a halt when several shells, probably from a Union battery on the little round top, screamed overhead and exploded not far away. Seth assumed the cannoneers on the hill had spotted the reb line that had passed by him recently and were warning them not to try another charge. The shells electrified the doctor and the stretcher bearers from the ambulances.

"Pick up these men and take them away quickly, before they become dead soldiers instead of wounded ones," the doctor yelled. The stretcher bearers worked feverishly to obey his order, roughly loading the wounded rebs into the wagons. "Hurry, hurry," the doctor pressed.

When the wounded were packed into the wagons—and their groans attested to the tight fit— the stretcher bearers and the doctor climbed aboard and drove the horses at a gallop back in the direction from which they—and Seth earlier—had come. "Thanks, rebel bastards," Seth yelled after them.

He heard the whiz of other shells. These burst somewhere east of his location, probably close to the aptly named Devil's Den. *If the doctor is right and I'm going to live,* Seth reasoned, *it doesn't make sense to risk being killed by friendly fire.* He raised himself to an upright position by sliding his back up the tree. He began to shuffle slowly toward the big round top, perhaps 200 yards ahead.

As before, the walking was both painful and exhausting, and he sunk to the ground panting. At least he was away from the shelling, Seth thought, although he still didn't know if he was really heading to the rebels' rear. "To hell with it," he said out loud and curled up with his head on his right arm. He slept the sleep of a baby. The morphine had at last kicked in.

When he awoke, he crawled to a tree and pulled himself up to a sitting position. As his eyes focused, he was looking past the big hill and more to the west. He noticed that the terrain on the other side of the valley was not as steep here as it had been when he made his observation at the stone wall. *Maybe that's the rear,* Seth thought, *up that slope.* Of course. The rebs had come at the Orange Blossoms from the west, down that ridge, into the valley, and up to and over the stone wall at the foot of the farmer's field. West is the rear.

He got up and headed toward the distant ridge. He had gone perhaps fifty yards when he tripped on a root and fell forward into Plum Run, which in July varied from shallow to merely dampness. Here it was soaking deep. "Sweet Jesus," he exclaimed, as he turned over on his back, pulled up his jacket, and allowed the water to cool the fire that clung to the hole in his back.

Dearest Yank, it's so hot here that some of us Dutch girls went wading in the pond behind grandfather's house. Seth knew the girls and he could see them all with their skirts pulled up. *Grandfather came out of the house and scolded us for exposing our legs. He threatened to fetch Domine Petrus Ackerman, who, he said, would tell us we were tempting Satan.*

Seth giggled to himself imagining the scene. He knew Grandfather Vandergost, a man of considerable girth, as big around as some of those boulders atop Devil's Den. He spoke Dutch more than English and still smoked one of those long clay pipes. He told stories, and it was difficult to know which were true and which were legend, or if they were some kind of hybrid; grandfather wouldn't let on what was what. His favorite tale was about Claudius Smith, whom he called the Cowboy of the Ramapos — the mountains south of Goshen that bumped east until they broke off and descended almost straight down into the Hudson River. Seth knew at least that Smith was for real, a diehard Tory during the Revolution whose fellow bandits — cowboys — raided the homes of patriots for several years before being captured and hanged. What Seth wasn't at all sure about was Grandfather Vandergost's claim that most of the loot collected by Smith and his gang was still hidden in caves and under rocks and roots of giant trees. "I know der his a map," the old man would announce at the end of the story in his broken English, "and vun of dees days I tell you where I tink it his. Den you find all dat treasure. You see." Of course, he never disclosed the map's location.

Seth sat up and splashed his face and head. By God, he thought, poor old Stretch Martin did smell water before he died. He looked north and south and saw that the stream meandered in both directions as far as he could see. It also branched off east not far from where he was puddling. Ever since he left the stone wall, he concluded, his trek must have paralleled Plum Run.

He suddenly sensed he was not alone. Two reb soldiers carrying a man on a stretcher were approaching from the southwest. "Sir, I think we finally found enough water in this here goddamned creek to fill one canteen and wet our whistles." The soldier spotted Seth. "Say, yank, you ain't movin' your bowels in that water are you?"

"No, johnnie, just cooling off. One of your doctors just gave me morphine. I was shot in the chest yesterday afternoon." Seth didn't want them to think he was a combatant in case they had firearms.

"Well, all right." The soldiers gently laid the stretcher on the ground by the stream. The man on the stretcher, evidently an officer, had his eyes closed and made no sound. His face was ashen. *I'm not going to say anything to these men,* Seth thought, *but my guess is that they're carrying a corpse.*

The soldier who had spoken to Seth filled his canteen and then bent over the still form on the stretcher and put the canteen to the officer's lips. There was no response and water dribbled down the man's chin and on to his jacket. "I think he may be unconscious, Sam. But he'll want a good swig once he wakes up. Let's take him on to the hospital." Sam said nothing, but he looked quickly at Seth, and it was plain in his eyes that he knew his officer was dead, but he didn't know how to deal with his friend's denial.

"Where you headin', yank?"

"To the rear."

"The rear of what?"

"Your lines."

"Then you got yourself a long hike. Most of our boys are way back there on the Emmitsburg Road and beyond. You might better strike out for a house and barn a little ways up the ridge there." He pointed to the long, gentle slope to the right of the base of the big hill. "I know for a fact there's yanks in there." He and Sam said no more, but picked up the stretcher and headed north along the stream.

A house. Out of the sun. Comrades. Well water. Maybe even food.

His brain was tingling every nerve and he mistook the feeling for energy. He crawled out of the stream bed and stood up slowly. *I can make that house,* he thought, *but it would help if I had something to lean on. Whatever happened to my musket? Did I leave it on the field where I fell, or did someone come along, probably a reb, and make off with it? I don't remember seeing it when I woke up this morning. In fact, I don't recall seeing any weapons on the ground since I set out. Maybe I can find a stout stick.*

He commenced searching. *I should have done this before,* he thought, *then I wouldn't have had to crawl so much.* He had almost given up when he spotted a branch about an inch thick and five or six feet long. He sat down, took out his knife and trimmed off the small shoots. He stood up again and put his weight on the stick. It bowed a little, but did not break.

Seth started up the slope in the direction the reb had pointed. The trees gave him shade, but the heat nevertheless soon replaced the cool dampness of the creek with sticky sweat and began to sap his strength. He had to sit down, and the house was not yet in sight. He got to wondering what time it was on this third of July. Mid to late morning, he guessed.

It also dawned on him that a week from today was his twenty-sixth birthday, his first away from home. "Oh, ma," he sighed out loud. For as long as he could remember, his mother had fussed over his birthday. A family picnic outdoors if it wasn't storming, usually on the bank of the Wallkill River, sometimes along the majestic Hudson. The Hudson River was his favorite. He wanted to build a house high on the cliffs overlooking the great river someday after the war where he and Goose would spend all their days together.

No matter where the picnic, there was always chocolate cake. "Choc-o-late cake." He said the words aloud, caressing each syllable. If we had stayed in camp down south, he mused, and ma had made a cake and sent it to me, I most likely would…. He forced himself to stop thinking about cake and picnics, ma and beloved Goose, the Hudson River and home.

He used the stick to raise himself to his feet, and the painful walk to the rear started anew. He eventually came out of the woods into an open field.

"Yowee," he yelled. Up ahead he could see what remained of a split rail fence long since taken apart by men of both armies, and beyond that a house and outbuildings. He almost ran. As it was, his wobbly pace quickened and his breathing was soon labored and his lungs and throat burned. "I'm not going to rest now," he said to himself, "not until I get inside that house. This is the end of the line for me."

Beyond the house, the ground ran out of slope and leveled off at the road to Emmitsburg, the very same one the Orange Blossoms had come up on the run just two days ago, when Ellis and Cromwell sat bold and anxious in their saddle and Stretch Martin dragged himself and his musket through dust that blotted out the sun's glare but not its heat. Arrayed along the ridge, with flags drooping because there was no breeze to catch their furls, were regiment upon regiment of the enemy, the southwestern terminus of the Army of Northern Virginia, which stretched north through the town and then curled east around Culp's Hill. Seth, in this third year of the war, still seldom referred to the rebels as the enemy. He had never been south, that is until last year when the 124th marched out of Washington and across the Potomac to Arlington Heights, Virginia, and he did not know a single man or woman south of the New Jersey border a day's ride from his home, but he guessed those pimply boys standing at ease along the ridge above him looked pretty much like young Angus McGregor, who lost his freckles and most of his head at Chancellorsville, and the wrinkled old men in butternut probably resembled hoary Hezekiah Peakes from Newburgh, who taught Seth how to roll a cigarette.

He moved slowly now, saving every ounce of strength. The house was made of fieldstone, one and a half stories. A porch extended from one corner of the house two-thirds of the way across the front. Its roof covered one of the two windows and the front door. Despite the trampling of hundreds of soldiers' boots and horses' hooves that had plastered down the fields of grain and plowed up most of the ground surrounding the house and outbuildings, in a tiny patch close to the house there bloomed summer flowers—daisies, hollyhocks, snapdragons. And alongside a building Seth assumed was the summer kitchen was an herb garden, its plants only partially picked over by hungry, desperate men.

Seth walked up the two steps to the porch, using the corner post to steady himself. He leaned his walking stick against the house and stood before the door. Should I knock, he wondered. No, the wounded soldiers inside might not be able to come to the door. Besides, knocking on the door somehow seemed to be too formal, too normal for a time when men who loved home and family put aside the rules of decent behavior made by God and man and tore at each other with bestial abandon.

He slowly opened the door.

CHAPTER TWO
Private Eldred Spencer

"Hello?"

"Arms over your head! Get 'em up. Now!"

"If I do, I'll fall down."

"Then fall down, mister. Or get felled by a bullet."

Seth turned to face the voice on his right. The voice belonged to a soldier sitting tall and straight in a rocking chair. He pointed a Colt revolver at Seth. The man's gun-powdered face seemed almost to blend into the blackness that surrounded his head from shaggy mane that covered his ears to the beard that curled as it fell to his chest.

Seth closed the door and sagged against it, his arms only partly raised from his sides. "What's the matter with you, comrade? I'm Federal same as you. One hundred twenty-fourth New York. For God's sake, look at my uniform. It's the same as yours."

"Don't mean shit, mister. Rebs steal everything off our boys, down to their goddamned underwear. You could be a reb spy sent to see who's here and what arms or food we might have that you johnnies could lay your dirty hands on. Ain't I right, boys?" The big head turned away and Seth's eyes followed.

He guessed the room to be twenty-five or more feet wide and perhaps fifteen or so feet deep. The parlor was to his left and the kitchen to his right, neither sliding doors nor an arch to separate the flow between them. A fireplace, with a single window alongside the chimney, was at either end; two windows in the rear, which Seth now faced, matched the location of the front windows. Bedding, evidently brought down from upstairs, was laid out in front of the parlor fireplace.

The "boys" were three in number. An older man, perhaps in his late forties or early fifties, stretched out on his back on a sofa against the opposite wall. The dried blood from his clumsily bandaged left knee had altered the pattern of the flowered upholstery. Dark red splotches created blooms where there were supposed to be leaves. He wore a mustache but no beard. His hands were stuck under suspenders and he appeared to be sleeping. At least he did not respond to the soldier with the revolver. Seated at the kitchen table playing cards by himself was a lad not out of his teens, but whose eyes had been aged by sights no youth should have to witness. He did not appear to be wounded, but Seth supposed his wounds could be hidden from view.

"Just as you say, Zinger," the lad said.

The third soldier sat in an upholstered chair by a table to Seth's left on which were framed pictures of a family, perhaps the owners of the house who had fled in haste when thousands of the blue and gray invaded their pastoral world. The soldier was clean shaven, except for a day-old growth; he was smiling and smoking a meerschaum. The man's right leg was propped up on a chair from the kitchen table and the trousers were torn, revealing an ugly gash that laid open the shin bone. It did not appear to have been treated. Like the man on the sofa, this soldier said nothing. He did not even look toward the giant the youth had called Zinger. He just kept smiling. What was there to smile about, Seth wondered.

"Prove to us you're not a goddamned johnnie," Zinger demanded. "I ain't foolin' about making you a fuckin' eunuch, ya know."

"I'm sure you're not, but how do I prove I'm one of you?"

The man in the upholstered chair spoke. "What was your unit?"

"One hundred twenty-fourth New York. How about you?"

"Seventeenth Maine. Name your officers. Quickly!"

"Colonel Ellis, Lieutenant Colonel Cummins…"

"First names. Quickly."

A Van Horne Ellis, F.M. Cummins—I don't know for sure what the initials stand for— Major James Cromwell. Let's see, David Crist— Captain Crist—commanded my Company H. Going down the line— er—a—Charles Wood, Company E and…"

"That's enough. I find this man to be a Federal soldier, Zinger. Put your revolver down. And clean up your language, please. It's offensive. Welcome 124th New York. Pardon me for not rising to greet you. Where are you wounded?"

"In the chest. A minie ball. Thank God it missed my heart, although I think maybe it nicked my lung here on the right side. I don't breathe too good. What about everyone else? Looks like you got really skinned by a piece of shrapnel or boulder."

"Hold on, hold on," Zinger interrupted. "Who the hell made you commander here, Spenser. You're only a stinkin' private like me. The only man here to hold any rank is the old man, and he ain't nothin' but a sergeant. This here soldier could be making up all them names. What does that prove? Now, I say…"

"Shut up, Zinger." The old man had opened his eyes and turned his head. "Since you mention it, I am a sergeant. And I also am satisfied that this man is telling the truth. Besides, if he was Confederate, why wouldn't he come in with a weapon and take whatever he wanted? Do you really think you'd be a match for him, you with a spine that won't even let you bend at the waist?"

"I got my revolver always ready, Sarge. I could drop anybody entering that door before he had a chance to fire. Right, boy?" He looked to the youth.

"You're ready all right, Zinger. Yes siree."

The old man sat up very slowly, holding the bandaged knee with his hands. "No telling how long we'll be here, 124th, so you might as well get to know who you're living with. I'm Horace Jenkins of the Third Michigan. Not many of us left, I expect. We got cut up badly. Somebody stuck me with his bayonet late yesterday afternoon. He pointed to the man in the upholstered chair. "Tell him about yourself, Spenser."

The man, still smiling, took the pipe out of his mouth. "Eldred Spenser, late of the Seventeenth Maine. I think I already told you that. I say 'late' because I think I'm a goner unless a surgeon gets to this leg before the Almighty and Satan commence to fight for my soul. What's your name, 124th?"

"Seth Adams, Corporal. From Walden, Orange County. Pretty country. Not far from the Hudson River and West Point." He turned to Zinger. "Is that your given name, Zinger?"

"Course not. Who the hell would call their son Zinger. I got that name from my friends when they seen the way I picked off rebs. Zing, zing. Two less rebs. You heard tell of Berdan's Sharpshooters, haven't you Adams? Only the best goddamned unit in the goddamned Army of the Potomac. My name is Zook, Lionel Zook. But if you call me Lionel, I'll plug enough holes in you that the burying squad'll think you was a slice of swiss cheese. Right, boy?"

"You mean what you say, Zinger. That's for sure. For darn sure."

"And what about you, son?" Seth addressed the young man.

"Davey Kinkaid, 115th Pennsylvania. And we seen more action than anybody yesterday."

"Well, I was near the Devil's Den, and we saw a hell of a lot of action, too. Where were you wounded, Davey?"

He took a deep breath. "Well, I wasn't wounded, although the bullets whizzed all around me. Then the rebs overrun the line. I stood my ground while everybody else fled. Stead of shootin' me, the rebs captured me."

"How did you get here?"

"I escaped. Right from under their eyes. They shot at me as I ran away, but they missed. I found this house and, well, here I am."

"You men are aware, I guess, that the rebs know you're here. It was them that pointed to this house and said I'd find wounded yanks."

"We know that, Adams." Jenkins was slouching on the sofa, rubbing his chest with his right hand. "But they don't bother us, and of course we can't bother them—Zinger notwithstanding."

"Why don't they send over a doctor?"

"Too busy with their own wounded, I reckon."

"They also know we'll kill 'em." Zinger waved his cocked revolver.

"Will you stop, Lionel." Spenser stared back at Zinger—daggers against daggers. "The war is over for us. Maybe for the country. It's been mighty quiet this morning. Maybe everyone's gone home. To New York, Michigan and Maine; and Virginia, North Carolina and Texas."

"I don't think so," argued Zinger. "Somethin's brewin'. I can feel it. I can smell it. Goddammit, I wish I could get out there and find me some rebs. Zing, zing, zing."

"I'd go with you in a minute, Zinger. Yes, I would." The boy's pale, blotchy face lit up.

"You two make me sick to my stomach. Is that all you can think of—killing? Haven't the last two and a half years sated your appetite?" Spenser puffed furiously on his pipe, the smoke hanging in little clouds along the ceiling.

Seth recounted what he had seen on the ridge, the rebel army standing down, but perhaps waiting either to attack as they had yesterday or to be attacked. Seth doubted the latter possibility. The union army was too well situated on the opposite ridge anchored by the little round top and a cemetery up near town. Why would they give up their own excellent defensive position to go up against the rebs' equally good position? Asinine generals might be so foolhardy, Seth thought, but he and the rest of the Army of the Potomac dearly hoped the army had at last been purged of the do-nothings and do-wrongs who had misguided the Union forces since 1861.

"Tomorrow's the Fourth of July," Jenkins almost whispered .

"That's right," Seth said. He was seated now on a chair opposite Kinkaid at the table. "I forgot. Should we do something, say something? If we're still here, that is."

"Oh, I guess we'll be here," the older man replied. "I reckon we could all sing the 'Battle Hymn' if everybody knows the words. Or..." He paused.

"Or what?"

"Or I could recite a little of the Declaration. I memorized the whole thing once. I can't recall most of it now, but I could start it off."

"The best way to celebrate is to destroy the Army of Northern Virginia," Zinger joined in. "And I mean destroy the bastards. Beat the living shit out of them. Then, the sons of bitches who started this war and sit on their fat, gentlemanly asses in Richmond would give up and let the south come back into the Union. Course, we might not make it that easy for them." He laughed.

"Wadda you mean, Zinger?" Kinkaid obliged. As usual.

"I mean that after old Jeff Davis surrendered, we'd hang him and his whole fuckin' Confederate cabinet. And maybe even put foxy Lee in front of a firing squad. Zing."

It was Spenser's turn. "Zinger, I see that you're a man who believes in justice. Suppose—just supposing, now—that the reason we haven't heard much noise today is because our army has skedaddled back toward Washington or, worse, has been beaten. Lee takes his victorious army down Pennsylvania Avenue in Washington, drags Lincoln out of the White House, accords him a five minute trial, and then hangs him from the nearest lamppost. Justice? We invaded the south, remember. Does justice belong only to the victor? Is it simply one of the spoils of war? The victors can loot a city, for example, because they're entitled. Right?"

"You're twisting everything," Kinkaid interjected. "That ain't fair to Zinger."

"Quiet, boy. What do you say, Lionel Zook, private, Berdan's Sharpshooters?"

"I say that I never killed one of my own, not even some of the rotten officers who wasted my comrades like they was sheep or somethin', but I just might zing you, especially if you don't stop calling me Lionel. And the answer to your stupid question is no...I mean yes...the winning side has a right to do whatever the hell they want. Okay?"

"Okay. There you have it fellow invalids, the classical definition of justice as set forth by that great American, Lionel—excuse me—Zinger Zook. Say, I like that alliteration."

"You callin' me names, Spenser?"

"No, Zinger. Forget it."

Eldred Spenser, aged 31 and one of the few enlisted men in all the ranks to have attended college (Colby, 1851-52), had been editor and chief reporter for a small but scrappy weekly newspaper in Bath, Maine, where the Kennebec River flows into the ocean. He believed in the

Union — always had — but when the war started, his reporter's skepticism bordering on cynicism questioned whether Lincoln and some of the hotter heads in the Republican Party had provoked hostilities by telling the garrison at Fort Sumter to, in effect, thumb their collective nose — and, not incidentally, point their cannons — in the direction of Charleston in what those southern people thought was their new country. Not that the Confederate States of America was or is legitimately their country, of course. He had written an editorial at the time, which the paper printed, perhaps with misgivings, because the publisher received some pretty nasty letters in response and almost got punched in the nose one day when he came out of the barber shop. The editorial criticized Lincoln and his administration for not withdrawing the garrisons at Fort Sumter and from other forts in the CSA until such time as "intense but cordial negotiations might first repair and reinforce the spiritual bond between the people of North and South so that ultimately the Union itself would be saved and then sustained for the benefit of Americans in every region."

Spenser's honest doubt about the necessity for conflict had turned to downright anger a year later when General McClellan collected considerably more men in blue than were now hunkered down there at Gettysburg and arrayed them grandly and almost literally before the gates to Richmond, but failed, either out of ineptitude or cold feet, to defeat the vastly smaller Confederate army, capture Richmond and probably end the war. Since McClellan's failure — and those of succeeding generals — the only fruits of the battles waged by the Union armies, as far as Spenser had been able determine, were bitter: young men who came home to Maine in pine boxes or missing an arm or a leg, dispirited and broken, their faces creased and their eyes glazed — already old men.

For these reasons, Spenser had resisted all the early importuning by federal and state governments to enlist, but finally and reluctantly he had concluded that the only way now to reunite the nation was to defeat the Confederate armies wherever and whenever they assembled for battle. That meant killing and wounding thousands of men from river towns like Bath and from little villages and farms that were not all that dissimilar from those that hugged the jagged and jutting coast of Maine and lay scattered like unnatural growths among its deep forests carpeted in white pine and birch . But he didn't have to like it, and he didn't have to suffer goons like Zinger who rejoiced every time his sharpshooter's bullet splattered gray-clad flesh and bone.

"Do you mind if I change the subject to food. I haven't eaten since yesterday. Is there anything here?" Seth directed his question to no one in particular.

"By God," said Jenkins, "believe it or not, none of us has looked. I guess most of us was hurting pretty bad when we got here and then we slept. Except for poor Zinger. He's twisted his back somehow and is afraid to move out of the rocking chair."

"How did he get in the rocker in the first place?"

"Dragged himself into it. Screamin' all the way. Right, Zinger? Tell him yourself."

"Us sharpshooters were put right here on this property early yesterday. I was behind a goddamned wall not more than fifty yards from the house. In the afternoon, we got pushed back by Longstreet's whole fuckin' army. Except me. I fell over one of those goddamned boulders that's all over the place and did something to my back. Couldn't stand. Couldn't hardly move. So Petey Furbush grabbed me under the shoulders and dragged me in here. Then he skedaddled. That's it."

"Kinkaid, you're not wounded. How come you haven't checked for food?"

Spenser answered for the youth. "I have a hunch that Private Kinkaid has been well fed. And recently. As I recall, he walked in here chewing on something. What was that, Kinkaid?"

"Not much. Not much at all. I found a piece of meat lying on the ground near somebody's camp fire. It weren't even tasty."

"Do you mind if I look around?" Seth stood up. It was an effort. He still had trouble breathing, and he grabbed the edge of the table when the room began to spin. Kinkaid came over to support him. "I'll help you," the boy offered.

"My guess, Kinkaid, is that the family who lived here left in a hurry.

They couldn't have taken all their food with them, I don't think. Tell you what. You check the summer kitchen and the cellar. I'll look around here." Kinkaid went outside.

Seth used his chair as a kind of walking cane and began a search of the kitchen. He first spotted a large earthen jar in a corner, took off the lid and hollered, "Potatoes, beans and carrots! We can fix a meatless stew."

The others watched his every move. "Adams, see that tin on the mantle," Jenkins shouted. "May be bread."

"Or a pie." Zinger licked his lips.

"It's bread all right. And not too stale."

"Jam. For God's sake, look for jam." It was Spenser's turn. "I haven't had bread with jam on it since I left home a year ago."

Seth ambled over to a corner cabinet to the right of the fireplace. He took a glass jar off the second shelf. "You're in luck, Spenser. It looks like jam. Wait, I'll taste it." He dipped his finger into the jar. "Apple butter, I think. Figures. They grow a lot of apples around here."

"Well, hurry up. Dish it out. Come on, Adams."

"Give me a chance to find a spoon or knife, will you."

"In the cupboard drawer," Zinger yelled. "Try the fuckin' drawer."

Seth pulled out the drawer and found flatware. Cups and dishes were on a shelf. "Wow, men, we're going to eat in style. When Kinkaid comes back, he and I can take some potatoes and vegetables out to the summer kitchen, put them in a pot, start a fire and—praise God—stew. And, of course, the bread and the apple butter."

"There's gotta be a well for water," Jenkins volunteered.

"Cider. I bet there's cider, with all them apples," Zinger said. "Look for a jug, man."

Just then, Kinkaid burst through the door. In one hand was a ham and in the other a sack. "God Almighty, I found heaven on earth."

"What's in the sack?"

"Peaches."

"Find any cider?"

"No."

"Shit."

"Here, Kinkaid." Seth handed him a bucket. "Get us some water from the well." The youth went out again.

"I wonder how the rebs, or some of our boys, missed the ham," Jenkins said. "Foragers aren't what they used to be."

"No one's had much time for foraging since the day before yesterday," said Spenser. "Besides, maybe the owners of this house were here until yesterday when all hell broke out on this piece of lovely Pennsylvania countryside."

Kinkaid rushed in carrying the bucket of water. "Somethin's goin' on, somethin's goin' on and it's big, mighty big." He was almost breathless.

"What you talking about, boy?" Zinger picked up the revolver off his lap.

"I don't rightly know, 'cept there's a heap of noise off in the distance. Like a lot of cannon and men moving somewhere."

"Where?"

"How am I supposed to know."

"I don't hear no shooting."

"I told you, Zinger. It's movement. Just a lot of movement."

"Could be the Army of Northern Virginia on its way to Washington. What do you think, Zinger?"

"What I think is that maybe you're a reb in blue. A goddamned traitor. What do you say to that, Spenser?"

"I don't say anything, Zinger. If you want to match war records with me, I'll be happy to oblige. The others here can be the judges. But I don't mean a body count. I mean just loyal service to the nation."

Spencer hiked himself up in his chair, which also moved the wounded leg slightly, and he winced at the pain. He was hoping Zinger either would brag at length about his skill at killing, which everyone, except Kinkaid the toady, would find revolting, or he would dismiss the taunt with some vulgarism or epithet, which would further disgust Jenkins, who gave evidence of being a very religious man. If Zinger was not true to form and simply recounted his army service since enlisting at the start of the war in Berdan's elite and much decorated unit, he would certainly show up Spenser. It was a gamble, but not much of one. As it turned out, he was right.

"Why don't you two cut it out," Jenkins interrupted. "Let's get on with the banquet."

"I agree," said Seth. "Who can peel potatoes?" Jenkins raised his hand and Kinkaid took some to him in a bowl Seth had set out on the table. "Okay, how about the beans and carrots?" Without waiting for an answer, he had Kinkaid take them to Spenser. "I'll slice the bread and fry some ham out in the summer kitchen. Kinkaid, please go start a fire." The young man left.

"I'm sure we're all going to be ravenous when the food is ready," said Jenkins. "Therefore, I'd like to say grace now."

"Say what?" Zinger asked.

"Grace is when you thank the Almighty for your food and other blessings he's sent your way."

"I ain't sayin' no grace. First, I don't know whether Adams here knows what the hell he's doin' and, second, no Almighty has sent me no blessings since I can't remember when."

"If I had a blackboard, Zinger," Spenser said with a smile, "I'd try my damndest to parse that sentence. You'll note that I said 'try'."

"Go fuck yourself. Com'on, Adams, get the food ready."

As if that exchange had never taken place, Jenkins leaned forward, with hands held together, and began in a loud voice, "God in heaven, thank you for providing this food we are about to eat. We pray that it will nourish our bodies even as we pray that the Holy Spirit will nourish our souls. Thank you, too, for bringing us through the battle. We also pray that you will lead to this house those who might be able to properly attend to our wounds. In the name of Jesus Christ our savior…"

Only Zinger did not join in the chorus of "Amen."

The summer kitchen to which Kinkaid and Seth repaired was located 20 feet northeast of the house, 20 feet Seth wished he had not attempted. He carried ham in one hand and bread in the other and wobbled slowly and heavily down the few steps off the porch and was already exhausted. He took a deep, aching breath and called as loudly as he could for Kinkaid, who had gone ahead as directed to light a fire in the summer kitchen stove. Kinkaid came on the run, perhaps fearing that Seth was bawling an alarm. When he joined Seth, both men stood silently for a moment to listen to the sounds Kinkaid had heard earlier, and they agreed that Zinger's nose for battle might have twitched correctly. Something was brewing; something big by the racket being made by thousands of rebel feet, not a few of them shod in U.S. Government issue shoes ripped from dying and dead Federals, pounding dirt and clomping through farmers' flattened fields somewhere north of the house. The rebel regiments Seth had seen on the ridge south and west of the house when he approached earlier were still there, but they seemed to have withdrawn more toward the Emmitsburg Road and beyond. Seth reasoned they were being held in reserve for whatever violence was about to be unleashed by the always surprising and viciously cunning Lee. The clamor and rumble of many cannon being maneuvered rolled down the valley between the opposing armies, bounced off the forested dome of the big round top just east of the house and slammed into the men where they stood.

"We better see about lunch while we still have time," Seth said.

Kinkaid held Seth's right arm, his right hand closed on the hunk of ham like a vise clamped to a board.

"Do you want I should take the ham and bread?"

"No, just lead me to the kitchen."

They shuffled into the kitchen, a clapboard, whitewashed affair only large enough to contain the stove, whose exhaust pipe plugged into the chimney that also served a wide fireplace, and two long, rough-hewn tables along the side walls. Pots and pans of various sizes and configurations hung on the wall to the right of the fireplace, and a huge iron pot, which appeared not to have been used for a while, dangled from a hook driven into the chimney just above the hearth's opening. The only utensils, laid out neatly on one of the tables, were a large, wooden ladle and matching flat spoon, a knife made for cutting, a cleaver made for hacking up a side of beef or hog, and a two-pronged fork that could easily heft a slab of meat far weightier than the one Seth had brought with him from the house. On the other table were three clay bowls, a shallow pan and a cutting board.

The fire set by Kinkaid was about right for frying the ham in the pan Seth found on the table. While he tended to the cooking, the boy sliced the loaf of bread. They didn't speak, primarily because Seth was trying to conserve what energy he had left. He began wondering whether that reb doctor really knew anything about his kind of wound; then he quickly reminded himself that unless the doctor had just come on the scene he must have seen a number of wounds like Seth's. *But he said there wasn't much bleeding,* Seth thought. Suppose all the bleeding was internal; suppose the wound was still oozing into his chest and the cavity was filling up — would continue to fill until he choked on his own gore.

Goose's voice sounded in his head.

Dearest Yank: You've always been a worrywart. I can remember when you once stepped on a nail and the wound became infected and you felt sure you'd lose your foot, maybe the leg. And will you ever forget the time you ate three green apples in a row and how later when the gas from those apples blew up under your rib cage you thought sure your heart was about ready to bust. Come on, my darling, you're alive! Maybe you should be dead, probably would be if that reb had had better aim, but you're not, and, furthermore, I won't let you get out of marrying me as soon as the war's over. Oh mercy! The war may be over for you — probably is. I bet they send you home because of that wound. Now, what do you think of that, dear?

"Hey, Adams, ain't that ham done yet?"

"Huh?" The ham was a little more than done. "Shit! We forgot to bring a dish for the ham — or the bread. What'll we carry them in?"

"I could go back to the house and fetch something."

"By then the ham either will be charcoal if I leave it on the fire much longer or cold if I take it off and lay it on the table."

Kinkaid saved the day. He took a large — and not too clean — bandanna out of a back pocket, wrapped it around his right hand, then grabbed the pan off the fire and tossed the bread slices on top of the ham. "Let's go."

Seth took hold of Kinkaid's left arm and together they reshuffled back to the house.

The movement of men and the machinery of war evidently had ceased, they thought, because an eerie, ominous silence had descended upon the valley of yesterday's death and the great armies that eyed each other malevolently from the ridges that bordered the valley. Seth wondered if Zinger's nose still picked up the scent of impending battle or whether perhaps the little hairs in his nostrils had simply been tickled by a wisp of dust.

CHAPTER THREE
Lorannah Vandergost

All agreed—even Zinger—that the meal was a twofold success. It returned strength to their bodies and raised their spirits.

It also made them sleepy.

Jenkins reclined again on the sofa and Zinger tried to doze in the rocking chair. With Kinkaid's help, Spenser moved to his mattress on the floor. The gash in his leg was bothering him more. Again with Kinkaid's help, Seth lay down on the other mattress. After assisting the others, Kinkaid curled up on the carpet in the parlor at the foot of the mattresses.

As Seth lay on his back with his head on a pillow, he was aware of a hissing sound. It occurred to him that air might be escaping from somewhere in his body. Nothing I can do, he thought, but try as hard as I can to stay alive until a doctor looks me over and does what has to be done. The same with the other boys. Right now, we need to concentrate on staying alive.

As he started to drift off, his mind conjured up a scene that was familiar and comforting. It was Storm King Mountain towering over and jutting out into a bend in the Hudson River above West Point. He saw it as he had often seen it as a boy on a summer's day when the humidity dropped a thin veil over the blue granite and great, green trees.

It had been a day's outing to go from his home in Walden to Storm

41

King and the river, where his family and friends swam and picnicked and watched the heavily-laden ships glide upriver to Poughkeepsie and Albany.

He would float on his back in the river and look up at the mountain, which always seemed like a huge beast, friendly to everyone who loved it and the Empire State, but crouched on the river's shore to stand guard against any who would try to invade the Catskills and the mighty Adirondacks further north.

He recalled now the July afternoon in the year before the war and all the bad days that followed. He and Lorannah and his friend Jed and his girl climbed to the top of Storm King. As they sat on the edge of a cliff to eat fried chicken and drink cold tea, they could pretty much see the outer limits of their world. None of them had been to Albany or New York City, and none had ventured as far as the southern borders with New Jersey and Pennsylvania. Only Jed's girl, Linda, had even crossed the river, to visit her mother's parents near Danbury, Connecticut.

"Did you ever see anything like it?" Linda exclaimed.

"It would take us two days—maybe more—just to reach as far as we can see," said Lorannah.

"Well, it ain't far enough for me." Jed stood up and swept his arm in a circle. "I want to see more. Maybe, if I'm lucky, all the way to California. How about that?"

He got as far as Chancellorsville, Virginia, where his body still rested.

Lorannah. She of the hazel eyes that revealed all and saw all. Gazing into those eyes, which he often did that long, pleasant summer of 1860 until he made her feel uncomfortable ("Why do you keep staring at me so?"), Seth discovered feelings not always expressed and thoughts not always declared. On one occasion he had unthinkingly and carelessly called her stupid, meaning only that she had missed some point in their conversation that Seth assumed was obvious. Before he could get new words out of his mouth to explain more precisely and considerately his point, her eyes disclosed the hurt he had inflicted.

Her eyes also penetrated facade and were as sensitive to pretense as most persons' eyes are to bright light. More often than he cared to admit, even now, he had concocted little scenarios in which he rehearsed what he would say and do and how she would respond. When his dream expectations fell short — and of course Lorannah had no idea what they were — he was terribly disappointed, not that he had any right to be. Naturally, he pretended he was not disappointed, but Lorannah immediately saw through his carefully constructed front and pressed him hard until he blurted out the scenario and an apology. Especially now that they were engaged, he could hide nothing from her no matter how carefully he tried to conceal his thoughts or feelings. "You always give yourself away, Seth, by a glint in your eye — or how you try to avoid my glance by looking maybe just a hair's width to one side or another — the way you square your shoulders, move your feet."

After lunch on that same July afternoon in 1860, Seth and Lorannah separated from Jed and Linda and walked hand in hand to a favorite spot that provided a clearer view of the river snaking through the mountains to the north. They found a smooth boulder, sat down, and waited in silence as the day added a microtick to the eons that had formed this mountain and river they loved so much. Still not speaking, they turned toward each other and simultaneously read what was on the other's heart. Lorannah ever so slowly lay back on the boulder on her right side facing Seth, her right arm cocked under her so that her open hand supported her head draped in long, black curls; she extended her left arm toward Seth, who lay down on his left side and grabbed her proffered hand.

Seth's courting of Lorannah, up until that moment, had consisted primarily of suppers at her house or his; an occasional, chaperoned dance at the Grange hall, and two other picnics with Jed and Linda. They had kissed only once, and in truth it was more a case of his lips brushing her cheek than a bona fide smooch. Now, facing each other, their eyes locked — hazel to hazel —and their hands clasped tightly, they felt for the first time sex hormones surging through their bodies faster and with greater force than the mighty Hudson coursing at flood tide.

Through the ages, lovers have looked back on their first sexual encounter usually with a remembered passion never quite surpassed thereafter and, at the same time, a certain embarrassment at how clumsily and awkwardly they approached intimacy. Three years after just such an event, and lying on his bed of pain at Gettysburg, Seth's memory of that afternoon was vivid enough to cause his heart to tighten and his penis to harden.

Looking deep into Lorannah's eyes, Seth saw an invitation to make love slowly and gently. She made the opening move by drawing their clasped hands toward her chest. Seth inched his body forward to follow his hand until he was close enough to inhale the rose-scented cologne Lorannah had splashed behind her ears and on her long, white neck that morning and to smell their lunch of fried chicken on her breath. She released his right hand, and together with his left he cupped her face and kissed her full on the lips, but tenderly, not hard enough to press them against her teeth. When he opened his eyes and gazed into hers once more, they spoke of surrender, sweet submissiveness.

Seth knew perfectly well, of course, where Lorannah's girlish breasts and virginal vagina were located, but he wasn't entirely sure how to get to them. He had no sisters, and his mother had never dressed or undressed in his presence. *I don't want to make a fool of myself,* he thought, *but exactly how do I arrive at bare skin, and where do I start?* He wondered what layers lurked beneath Lorannah's dark, red skirt that billowed over the boulder like a giant plum stain.

Lorannah rolled over on her back. Then, as if sensing his dilemma, she took his right hand, placed it at her throat, and then guided it beneath her blouse until it came in contact with her bodice. She guessed he could figure out what to do from there. And he did. He had never felt anything so warm and soft as Lorannah's breasts, which rose and fell ever faster at his touch, especially when he caressed the nipples smoothly and lightly, so that they popped up between his fingers like a cow's teats at milking time. His movements almost belied his innocence and lack of experience as a lover.

Later, his hand went under Lorannah's skirt and up her leg, but before he could pull down her undergarments, let alone touch her vagina, he ejaculated into his pants like every other rank amateur. The dalliance — more beautiful and arousing then either partner had ever imagined — was at an end.

Their passion for one another had overwhelmed their pre-marital common sense on two or three occasions since then, but the sensation was never quite so powerful as that first time. Seth doubted that moment three years ago would ever be equaled.

Dearest Goose: I was just remembering how we made love on the boulder at Storm King. Oh, how wonderful it was! I must have loved you even then. I know I love you desperately now — still — and the miles between us have only made me hunger all the more to feel your embrace and see the lights dancing in your eyes.

Dearest Yank: I remember, too, and the fire you kindled when you were home still smolders and can be brought to flame by your touch, even your glance. I don't know where you are now, but I am afraid for you. Just a little, though, because I know God watches over you — at least I've asked him to. I love you, Seth.

Slowly, the memory of that summer's afternoon faded and the mist over Storm King became a curtain that finally descended, and Seth fell asleep.

No one, including Zinger, who slumped in his rocking chair when the excruciating pain along his spine let up, heard the rapid boom-boom from Miller's battery of the Washington Artillery, the pride of New Orleans, that, exactly at one o'clock signaled the greatest artillery duel of the Civil War. But the crash of 138 Confederate cannon and 85 answering Union guns that followed shook the house, assaulted their ears and jolted everyone awake.

Seth rolled off his mattress, became disoriented and was now crawling aimlessly on the floor.

Zinger had jerked straight up at the terrible racket and now screamed as the pain returned to his back full force. "Davey, here take my revolver. Put a fuckin' bullet through my brain, cause I can't stand this any longer. Do it, boy." He handed the gun to the youth.

"You crazy, Zinger? I couldn't kill you. Never, never. Why, I ain't killed anybody. I ain't even fired a gun."

Zinger's gaze was both quizzical and accusing. "You mean in this whole goddamned war you never pulled the trigger, never shot nobody? You—you're a…goddammit, Davey, are you a coward?"

"No, Zinger. I'm no coward. I were jus' scared. I ain't like you, Zinger. I'm 'fraid to kill and 'fraid I'd be killed. But I ain't no coward."

"The hell you're not. Down deep you're plain yellow. I can see the yellow now shining beneath that blue uniform you've disgraced. Your job was to kill the rebs as fast as you could. Your comrades depended on you, goddammit. I oughta shoot you myself. Right now."

"Please, Zinger, don't call me no coward, and for God's sake, don't wave that gun at me." The boy started to cry.

"Get away from me, Davey. Get away. Coward, coward, coward…" He interrupted himself with another scream as a thousand knives dug into his back.

"What's going on?" Spenser yelled to be heard above the din of cannon blazing away at each other across tranquil farmer's fields, where the ripening grain stalks stretched their nodding heads toward a sun that had been almost obliterated by the giant blanket of acrid smoke that spread in all directions. Spenser stood up with difficulty and limped into the parlor, dragging his torn and swelling leg.

"Kinkaid, can you help me over to the chair?"

Kinkaid had pulled back from Zinger and was leaning against the rear wall, sobbing.

"It's all right, boy." Spenser tried to reassure the youth. "Noise won't hurt you, no matter how awful."

"It ain't the noise that's botherin' him," said Zinger. "He just found out that he's a goddamn coward. Never fired his gun. Can you believe it?"

"What is it with you, Zinger. Must you hate everyone? Is it not enough that you actually enjoy killing your fellow Americans in gray? Now you turn your hate against a lad that shouldn't even be here. He should be milking a cow, or skimming rocks on a lake or making love to a girl. Not here. Not forced to kill or be killed. Leave him alone, for God's sake. Leave him alone, or I'll…"

"Or what, Spenser? You're not much better than him, ya know. Always talking about the goddamned rebs as if they weren't our sworn enemy. I should zing the both of you. But, I, like a good yankee—maybe the only one in this house—I'm savin' my ammunition in case those rebs you like so much come stormin' in here."

Spenser reached the armchair by the table, sat down heavily and lifted his leg onto the other chair. He picked up his pipe, filled it with tobacco, lit it. He breathed in the fragrant smoke and let it out very, very slowly.

Jenkins was sitting up on the sofa, his hands over his ears, his eyes closed and his head shaking. Kinkaid, who was standing nearby wiping his eyes, thought he heard the old man singing. He leaned over to catch the words: "My hope is built on nothing less than Jesus' blood and righteousness; I dare not trust the sweetest frame, but wholly lean on Jesus' name. On Christ, the solid rock, I stand; all other ground is sinking sand, all other ground is sinking sand."

"Kinkaid, please." It was Seth still on his hands and knees.

"Okay, okay. I hear you." Kinkaid, whose face was now almost devoid of emotion, moved slowly toward Seth and held out his hand. Seth grabbed it and Kinkaid drew him up slowly and let him lean his weight on his shoulder. Kinkaid led Seth to the sofa where he collapsed alongside Jenkins.

The five men sat stunned and unmoving for an hour and a half as the thundering artillery hurled tons of iron back and forth between ridges. Then, as suddenly as the cannonade had begun, it stopped. In the loud silence, the men's ears popped and ceased ringing.

Kinkaid ran to the front door and opened it.

"Can you see anything, boy?" Jenkins was sitting on the edge of the sofa, rubbing his chest. It wasn't apparent to the others — yet, but it was dawning on Jenkins that his real war wound was not to his knee but to his heart. The forced march three days ago up from the vicinity of Taneytown, Maryland and the hard fighting yesterday — all endured under a sun that branded every inch of skin, exposed and unexposed, had strained arteries already clogged with forty-three years worth of absorbed animal fat; now they were making their host painfully aware of his abuse of them.

"I can't see nothin 'cept smoke, and I mean a cloud like none of us has ever seen before. It's kinda like the world's been turned upside down. There ain't no cloud in the sky; it's hugging the ground. Like I say — upside down."

"Do you hear anything?" Seth was trying to get up from the sofa. The jolt off the mattress had inflamed the in and out chest wounds and also the insides between the holes.

"I ain't sure. It sounds like…" Kinkaid's sentence was drowned out by another round of cannonading. This time all the noise and shells came from the east, some fairly close by from the guns on little round top. What Kinkaid could not see were forty-two Confederate regiments emerge from Pitzer and McMillan woods south of the Lutheran Seminary in a dressed line a mile long, flags hoisted in search of a breeze and bayonets flashing the sun backward toward their own generals and forward to their sworn enemy a mile away. Waiting behind stone walls. As the Union cannon continued to slash their ranks with canister, these men who thought of themselves as Lee's Invincibles commenced their long death march across the golden fields, soon to be red with their blood.

Finally, the cannon roared their last roar, only to be replaced by the din of muskets seeming to fire all at once. Then, above that noise of ten thousand firecrackers, rose a sound none of them had heard before. It was as though some giant animal — perhaps a dog as big as a mountain — had been struck down and now lay on its side, covering all the ground between the town of Gettysburg and the house where resided these wounded men, and the beast moaned so plaintively and loudly that anyone who heard it knew at once the animal was suffering terribly. The groan carried through the open front door, past Kinkaid, and filled all the rooms. It settled there for what seemed like hours, but in fact was slightly less than an hour, and then it was gone. But not forgotten. Each man knew for certain that that awful dirge had permanently taken up residence in his soul, where it could be heard whenever the days of war, and particularly July 3, 1863, were dredged up in memory.

Kinkaid closed the door and walked numbly past Zinger, who was sitting forward in his chair. The youth avoided looking at this one to whom he had foolishly toadied, this profane and vulgar killer. If he had, he would have seen a fervent longing—not for a hiding place, not for hearth and home, but a keen desire to be poised behind the wall on the Federal ridge waiting for the rebs to get so close he could see the bullets from his gun knock them down. Zing, zing. The killing played out in his eyes.

Kinkaid sat on the floor hunched against the back wall, his arms folded over his knees and his head resting on his arms. His face reported that he wished at that moment to be anywhere but in that house — in the company of these men, particularly the killing machine sitting by the door, who had so ferociously embarrassed him in front of the others. *If I had a gun or a knife, I'd kill Zinger for calling me a coward,* the boy thought, *but, no, I probably wouldn't. I just can't kill someone this close to me, not since I....* He buried again, deep in his subconscious, that moment during yesterday's battle when.....He refused to remember the moment.

A butternut blur crashed through the front door.

Zinger wailed, brought up his revolver and fired. Whoever it was that had burst into the room staggered a few feet toward Seth and Jenkins sitting wide-eyed on the sofa, then fell heavily face down on the floor. He did not move.

For a moment, no one breathed. Then, Seth and Jenkins almost simultaneously dropped to the floor and crawled toward the fallen Confederate soldier. Kinkaid snuffed up, unwrapped his body and also came to the reb's side.

Zinger, blowing the smoke from his revolver, regarded the scene with a killer's pride, but said nothing. Spenser stood on his good leg, his mouth open as if to say something, but no sound came forth. And then he yelled, "Zinger, you stupid, vicious bastard, what have you done?"

"Shut up, shut up. I was protecting you and the rest of these goddamned cowards. I was trained to kill rebs and I mean to take down as many as I can, especially when they come in here ready to do us harm."

"What harm?" It was Jenkins, who had assisted Seth in rolling the soldier onto his back. "This is a mere boy. Kinkaid, how old are you?"

"Eighteen. Almost."

"I don't think this lad is even that. What do you think, Adams?"

"About sixteen or seventeen, maybe. And, Zinger, he has no weapon. There is none on the floor and none I can find on his person."

"So, what was I supposed to do, check his age and whether he had a weapon? By that time he coulda killed all of us. I'm the sentry here, remember. None of you even have a gun. I got the only one, and I'm on guard duty twenty-four hours a day. You oughta be thanking me, you lousy ingrates."

"Is he dead?" Spenser asked. He had resumed his seat.

"No," Seth replied, "and I don't see a lot of blood, although there is a hole and powder burn I noticed in the back of his shirt before we turned him over."

"Is he conscious?" Spenser asked.

"No, and his breathing is labored, and his heart is racing."

"Shock," Jenkins said, he'd seen this before. A severe wound, and then falling headfirst on the floor. "He's in shock."

"Kinkaid, can you get us a little water?"

"I reckon." Kinkaid got to his feet slowly and went over to the bucket of water. "How's he gonna drink if he's unconscious, or are ya goin' to pour it over his face?"

"A little on his face for now," Jenkins answered. "He's very flushed."

"And grimy." Seth took a bandanna from the boy's pocket and soaked it in water. He wiped the face until freckles showed. He brushed straw-colored curls away from the boy's forehead and dripped water into his hair. "I have a brother no older than this. Papa wouldn't let him shoot pheasants let alone go to war."

"Check all his pockets," Zinger said. "Maybe he's a messenger. Or maybe a reb coward. They come in blue and gray, ya know." He looked toward Kinkaid, who averted his glance.

"His pants may be reb issue," said Jenkins, "but his shirt looks homespun. Nothin' at all in the shirt. Let's see about the pants pockets."

Jenkins stuck his hand in one side and Seth the other. "Nothin'," said Jenkins.

"I got a piece of paper, folded."

"I told ya. A messenger."

"I don't think so, Zinger. Not unless Lee or Longstreet is writing to this boy's mother."

"What's it say?" Spenser asked from across the room.

"The letter's dated June 30," Seth began. "'Dear Ma. In the north at last. Not sure where, but Pensilvanya. Eatin' ok for a change. Peaches and cherries. Ate so much got the runs. Sorry, ma. The boys brung in some catill and chickins and hogs other day. My, weren't that somthin. Pa and Jeremy are up front of me. I seed em just yestraday. Pa says there's goin to be a rootin tootin batill. You know pa. Jeremy can't hardly wait for the shootin' to begin. But I ain't so ankshus, ma. Do you think I'm scared? Not much more to say. Love to the litill ones and granny. And corse you too, ma. Love, Possum.'"

"Possum? What the hell kind of name is that?"

"What the hell kind of name is Zinger, Zinger? Probably the boy is — was — good at hunting possum down south." Spenser was puffing away and trying to lock eyes with Zinger so the latter could see and feel how much he loathed him.

"Look there," Kinkaid blurted. "See his legs and feet twitchin'. What's happenin'? What's that mean?"

"I don't know, boy." Jenkins studied the soldier's body. "Maybe rigor mortis. I saw a dead man jumping like that once. A regular Mexicani bean, if you know what I'm saying. But I really don't know. Has he stopped breathing, Seth?" It was the first time the older man had called Seth by his Christian name.

"No. And his heart is still beating."

"You'll see soon enough." A cloud covered Spenser's face. "The boy's paralyzed, I imagine. The bullet from Zinger's gun probably lodged in his spine. The twitch is nothing more than reflex. It's like rigor mortis, only the boy isn't dead. Just his legs and feet."

Kinkaid whistled softly through his teeth. "I think I'd rather be killed outright than not be able to move for the rest of my days. God, that's awful. He won't never even be able to mount a woman proper."

The child soldier moaned.

"He's coming to, I think." Seth put his hand under the lad's head and raised it slowly. "Boy, can you hear me?"

His eyes suddenly popped open and he tried to push himself up, but fell backwards. "Shelter, Jeremy," he mumbled. "Find shelter, for God's sake. Pa's dead. O ma, poor ma. Pa's dead. Shelter." He closed his eyes again.

"Sounds like he's talking about the brother in the letter," Zinger interrupted. "Maybe that Jeremy's outside with a gun ready to pick us off if we go to the door."

"And maybe Meade's going to walk in and pin a medal on you for gunning down a weaponless child." Spenser was back at his pipe. "If his brother is out there, he's either dead, wounded or frightened beyond comprehension. It's natural for every soldier to be scared, Zinger, to hope God Almighty has built a shield around him to protect him from that next bullet or shell fragment or bayonet. And for a boy, who had all those cannon aimed at him a while ago, who just lost his pa, well…"

"Another sermon from goddamn reverend Spenser. Davey, don't open the door, but peer out that window and see if you see anyone pointing a rifle at us."

"Let someone else do somethin' for a change. Besides, I ain't speakin' to you no more. Not after you called me a coward."

"You called him that, Zinger?" Seth, who was still on the floor with his hand under the Confederate's head, glanced up.

"So what if I did. He said he hadn't fired his gun in the whole war. Never. That's the mark of a coward in my book."

"And what's the mark of a hero, Zinger? In your book?"

"The soldier who does his duty."

"And the only duty is firing a gun?"

"Yesiree. You got it exactly, Adams."

"For starters, then, how about surgeons, one of whom may eventually set your back straight? How about all the soldiers who never get near the front, but unload supplies, guard prisoners and ammunition dumps?"

"Maybe they're doin' duty, but they'll never be heros. Never."

"No? I heard tell of a soldier who got the Medal of Honor for dodging bullets so's he could pick up the flag and drag its bearer behind our lines. He never fired at anyone. Not a single bullet."

"Go fuck, Adams."

"That's the way Zinger Zook always responds when he's been put in his place," said Spenser. "His mouth is an open sewer."

"One more time, Spenser, and…"

"And what? Got another bullet, do you, Zinger? Need to fire it at someone? Need to kill again? Go ahead and shoot me. Aim for my leg. That's going to come off anyway. But if you kill me, look around at the witnesses. They'll see you hang, or do you plan on killing everyone and then rock in that chair 'til you rot?"

"He's awake again." It was Jenkins. "Boy, can you hear me? Nobody here's going to hurt you." He glared up at Zinger from where he still sat on the floor. "Want water? Can you take a drink?"

"Jeremy. Where's Jeremy? Our pa's dead."

"I know, son. When was Jeremy with you?"

"The cannon ball. Took a big branch offen a tree." He suddenly sat up. "Run, Jeremy, run. Watch out, Jeremy!" He sank back. But he was still awake.

"There wasn't nobody with you," said Kinkaid, who peered into his enemy's face, which showed only tiny, thin hairs poking out here and there — an obviously failed attempt at growing a beard. "Are you sure your brother made it?"

"We went for shelter. He was behind me."

"They're both deserters," Zinger judged.

"Shut up, Zinger." They all said it at once.

Kinkaid, without being asked, went to the window. "I don't see nobody out there. The noise is still terrific, and the smoke up yonder is like a great storm gatherin'. Can't hardly tell it's daytime. You oughta be over there, Zinger. A pile of killin' goin' on for sure. Oh, I forgot, I ain't talking to you no more."

"What's your regiment, son?" Jenkins asked.

"Seventh South Carolina."

"Oh," Spenser sighed. "You boys came at us pretty good yesterday."

"You were in the thick of it, Spenser?" Zinger asked, almost unbelieving.

"Yes. Why does that surprise you, Zinger? And I fired my gun, and, God help me, I probably killed or wounded some of this boy's friends. I'm not proud of yesterday's work."

"I misjudged you, Spenser. You're not as bad a soldier as I thought you was."

"I don't want your admiration, Zinger. You like to kill; I don't. I regret it. I have nightmares. I feel guilt, and I seek God's forgiveness. But I don't think He ever will. Forgive me, I mean. I don't think He'll forgive very many of this generation of Americans who slew each other for causes most never understood in the first place."

"If you two will be still," Seth said, "perhaps we can do something for this boy so far from home, who now has to be told one more piece of very bad news. The third of this hellish day."

CHAPTER FOUR
Private Jefferson "Possum" McCall

A sixteen-year-old boy is supposed to cry, or at least whimper, when told he will never again race his friends to the swimming hole on a summer scorcher, will never walk hand-in-hand with his best girl through spring grass beneath fragrant boughs of apple blossoms. But not Jefferson McCall, the youngest—and perhaps only—son in a now fatherless family that had scratched a bare living from a scraggly dirt farm near Ulmer on the bank of the Salkehatchie River deep into South Carolina's innards. The boy was called Possum, because the first time his daddy took him hunting — the first time ever! — when he hoisted the rifle almost as long as he was tall and dug the stock into his bony shoulder and pulled the trigger, a plump possum hanging by his tail from an upper branch in an ancient pine riddled by woodpeckers dropped like a stone.

Possum's lower lip did bleed just a little, however, where he bit down on it after Seth and Jenkins asked if he could raise his legs and wiggle his toes and he had failed in his mighty effort to comply.

They decided not to move the boy for fear the bullet pressing against his spine might dislodge and cause even more damage. So he lay there on his back on the carpet, with a pillow under his head and his wet bandanna laid across his forehead, not far from the rocking chair and the man who had shot him and who was just beginning to have mixed thoughts about what he'd done.

Lionel Zinger Zook was not used to mixed thoughts. Enemies were and always would be enemies. Friends—well, he didn't trust anyone long enough nor hard enough to call him a friend. If an action or an idea were once judged by Zinger to be wrong, it would forever be wrong. No one could make it right. On the other hand, if Zinger judged something to be right, he could not be persuaded otherwise.

He never forgave and never sought forgiveness. His father had once knocked him to the ground with his fist because he was convinced Lionel had stolen money from his dresser. When the father discovered that his wife had taken the money to buy groceries, he went to Lionel, apologized profusely and tried to embrace him. Zinger ran from his father and thereafter punished him for his remaining days by speaking only when spoken to and by not giving nor accepting any sign of affection, no matter how slight. When his father died in his early forties, Zinger, then in his teens, went hunting on the day of the funeral.

Now, an infinitesimal fissure appeared in the hard shell that made Zinger a fearless warrior on the battlefield, but an unlovely and unloved human being. At first, Zinger didn't notice the crack in the facade, and neither did anyone else. It opened ever so slowly as he engaged Possum in a mostly one-sided conversation that consisted, at first, of bragging of his prowess as a sharpshooter, then an almost-apologetic defense of his shooting of the boy, and finally a rambling recital of the tribulations of his childhood and youth.

"Possum, huh? Of the Seventh South Carolina, huh?"

"Yes and yes. My Christian name is Jefferson."

"Not named for that traitor Jefferson Davis I hope?"

"You mean the president?"

"The one and only president is Abraham Lincoln, son. Remember that. Davis is nothing more than a goddamned traitor." Possum didn't retort. Zinger still held the only weapon. "Good thing you boys wasn't in front of me in yesterday's battle. Least I don't think you was there. No, I'm sure it was an Alabama regiment. They came out of some woods where we was waiting for 'em. Berdan's Sharpshooters. The Second Regiment. And we dropped them 'bama boys like an axe cuts down saplings. Zing, zing, zing. Every time I fired, a goddamned reb would hit the dirt. Course they was shootin' at us, and so it was fair and square, ya know. Guy next to me had his right eye and nose blown right offen his face. Ooooh, what a mess."

"If it's okay by you mister, I ain't so anxious to relive yesterday. Or today. Know what I mean?"

"Course, but you got to know how it was—how it is. Your army's got to be stopped."

"Stopped from doin' what?"

"Well, er—a—breaking up the United States. Secede, you call it. It's all that goddamned Jeff Davis' fault. We're gonna hang the sonofabitch when we catch him."

"Iffen you do."

"Oh we will, all right. Jus' wait an' see. You're lucky to be out of this war. You'd probably get killed eventually defending that no good…"

"I don't feel lucky."

"Well, that's because…tomorrow…some day, you'll…Say, do you know anything about Berdan's Sharpshooters? You musta heard about us. Everybody has."

"No, never did hear tell of that bunch."

"That bunch? Some bunch, I'd say. Jus' the best soldiers in the army, that's all. Let me tell you about us. Jus' listen up, boy." Possum's eyes were closed, but Zinger didn't notice. "We had to pass a fuckin' test, ya know. Had to get ten bullets in a row within fifty inches of a bull's-eye at a range of 200 yards. Lots of men couldn't do it. And the rest of the army—like these here in the house—didn't have to prove nothin'. Hell, three-quarters of 'em probably couldn't even find the target at 200 yards." Now he looked down at his prostrate enemy. "Hey, boy, you listenin' to me?"

Possum opened his eyes. "Oh, sure. Go right ahead, mister."

"Well, at first we was issued special uniforms. Dark green coat and light blue trousers. And we wore a green hat with a black plume. Mighty good lookin'. If we marched down a street, the girls would run out jus' to touch us and sometimes kiss us. I had a beautiful woman—in her twenties, I'd say—who come up to me and put her lips full on mine. I swear it. Well, now, that was early in the war. Our first duty once we gone south was…"

Possum shut out Zinger . He was already imagining being down south, sitting on the bank of the Salkehatchie waiting for a catfish to bite. As Zinger droned on, the boy saw himself dangling his hot feet in the cool, muddy water. The sensation went up from his feet until it reached his head, and for a moment it was almost like a breeze had drifted in from the faraway sea, caressed the coastal islands, negotiated the intestine-like curls of the Combahee River, puffed up the Salkehatchie and then, with just barely enough oompf left, pushed the heat that melted the day west to the Georgia border.

In his daydream, it was before the war. Life was hard on the family, but none of them courted an early death somewhere north in a land controlled by the hated yankees. They didn't know exactly why they hated yankees, but everybody on either muddy bank of the Salkehatchie, and even uncles and aunts and cousins living downriver where the long cotton was picked and then sold abroad to pay for the war and where rice and indigo had been harvested since colonial times, knew they were supposed to hate yankees, so they all did. Except they weren't altogether sure who or what yankees were. Did they all live in Washington and New York? Were they all fat, rich and lazy? Did they really love niggers all that much? And what did they want with poor southern folk anyway?

"Possum. Jefferson. Come here, son." The boy could hear his father call him from across the baked fields of corn and goober peas. "There's work to be done, Possum. Come on, now."

His papa was a kindly man who loved his family and the Lord. Possum knew that as well as he knew that yankees were evil and that niggers were content being what they were. But the boy also knew he had better go after the first call from his father. Any delay—more waiting on the catfish, more enjoying the imaginary sea breeze—was flirting with a scolding at best and a whipping with the stick by the back door of the house at worst.

"Possum. Jefferson McCall!" His eyes popped open.

"You're our prisoner, ya know." Zinger had leaned his gun-powdered face over the side of the chair and his eyes bore into the boy like the bullet that had ended every dream and passion Possum could remember feeling as he grew up on the farm near Ulmer and the river.

"That so?"

"Course it's so. Hey, you're not toyin' with me are you, boy?"

"Not me, mister."

"Well, okay." Zinger winced as he sat up straight in the chair and it rocked ever so slightly. "Goddamn back. I can't figure what makes it pain so. It never lets up."

"Somebody shoot you, too?"

"Hell no. None of you people has a bullet with my name on it. No sir, I ain't gonna die 'cause of no reb."

"I plum never thought a yankee would kill me, or pa, or Jeremy."

"You ain't dead, boy."

"Might jus' as well be."

"Say, that bullet you took could move one of these days and— zowie—you're up and movin' about like nothin' ever happened."

"You believe that, mister?"

"Oh sure. Don't you?" the boy didn't answer, so Zinger repeated his question, knowing full well in his heart of hard hearts that it was a cruel teaser.

Possum finally answered. "No." Again a long silence. "And, mister, you got no right makin' me suffer more than I oughta jus' thinkin' about the impossible."

Spenser was asleep, but Seth, Jenkins and Kinkaid, who had been engaged in conversation, paused long enough to hear this latest exchange between Zinger and the boy. The youth's voice had cracked mid-lament and the three of them looked into Zinger's dark face to read any sign of recognition that his wickedly false hope had hurt this boy almost as much as the bullet from his Colt revolver.

The others missed it, but Seth was sure Zinger blinked twice. That was all, but Seth would have sworn then and there if given a Bible on which to take the oath that the blinks held back a tear that probably had been under lock and key in some secret reservoir since Zinger was a babe in his mother's arms.

Seth and Jenkins continued to chat, but Kinkaid curled up on the carpet next to Possum and dozed off. The noise from the battle north of the house still resounded off the nearby hills and the distant Blue Ridge, although the earlier fury seemed to have dissipated some.

"I had to do it, ya know." Zinger's head rested against the back of the chair, and he stared straight ahead.

"Do what?"

"Shoot you. That's what."

"Why? I had no gun. I was jus' tryin' to get way from those yankee shells droppin' on us like apples back home when a big wind would take to shakin' the trees real hard like."

"I'm the guard here. I protect the others. We're wounded—well, they are—but we're still soldiers. For us, the battlefield just moved inside. Hear what I'm sayin', boy? If we was dug in behind a rock wall or behind trees, and you—or any other reb—came runnin' at us, don't you s'pose we'd fire at that reb? Don't you think we'd try to kill him before he killed us. We sure as hell ain't going to be lookin' to see whether he has a weapon. There ain't no time for that. Hell, when you crashed in here, how am I—the sentry—gonna know you was jus' scared and meanin' no harm." Zinger hesitated less than a second, but to Seth, who had cocked his ear in that direction again, it seemed much longer, and the moment seemed laden with an emotion that could be felt but not defined. "I couldn't have knowed you was jus' a boy."

"Would that have made a difference, Zinger?" Seth asked.

Zinger, caught off guard by the question, actually thought for a moment. "Maybe. I don't…" Then he was himself again. "Say, New Yorker, who asked you into this conversation?"

"I was just curious."

"Well, be curious about something else. How about you and Davey gettin' curious about findin' somethin' in this house that will kill this fuckin' pain in my back. It's actin' up somethin' fierce. A couple of swigs of whiskey or anything alcoholic will do. And maybe this reb could use somethin' to eat." He turned toward Possum. "When was the last time you ate, boy?"

"I ain't sure, what with all that's been goin' on, but I reckon it's been quite a spell."

"Well, we found a ham this mornin' and there's plenty left over. Adams, get the boy some ham while you're at it."

"You through giving orders, Zinger?"

"Maybe."

"Well, I'm through listening to them. But the boy—Possum—does need some food and drink. I'll see what Kinkaid and I can do about that."

Seth raised himself up slowly, then prodded Kinkaid lightly with his shoe. "Davey, help me get our guest some food, will you?"

Kinkaid rolled over on his back, stretched his limbs in all directions, then slowly went from sitting position to kneeling to standing. "I may have some more myself."

"Well, we got tonight, Davey, and tomorrow and who knows how long before someone comes to get us."

"Hey, I wonder if I went out I could find our lines and bring back a doctor."

"I wouldn't try it, Davey. Far as I know, we're still in the enemy's camp, so to speak. They might grab you and ship you off to a Richmond prison."

Kinkaid helped Seth to the table where the ham was covered by a damp cloth. Seth cut a slab and gave it to Kinkaid to hand to Possum. "Help him sit up, will you?" Seth said. "Gently. Very gently." Kinkaid raised up the boy. "Here's a cup of water." Seth passed it to Kinkaid.

"How about some whiskey, for God's sake." Desperation sounded in Zinger's voice.

"If this is a God-fearin' household, and I think it could be," said Jenkins, waving a Bible he had discovered earlier on a table next to the sofa, "then I doubt you'll find any spirits. A God-fearin' man toughs it out."

"I'm no goddamn God-fearin' man. Adams, look for the fuckin' whiskey."

"Zinger, your language is really offensive," Jenkins said. "Can you for once consider someone other than yourself."

"Go to hell, Bible-toter. Find the goddamn whiskey!"

"If you put it that way one more time," Seth replied, "I won't even

give you a spoonful of water when you ask for it. So, Mister
Sharpshooter of little boys, shut up!"

Zinger growled and then screamed as he tried to rise out of his
chair. He fell backwards, his face drained white under the battle grime.
He was silent.

With Kinkaid as support, Seth looked into several cabinets and found
no whiskey. Then he asked out loud to no one in particular, "If one
wanted to hide the demon, where would it be?"

"My daddy, who went to church real regular, used to hide a little
whiskey in the outhouse," Kinkaid offered. "Once in a while he'd slip
out to relieve himself and end up takin' a snort or two. He also carried
a little peppermint with him, so's Ma never could smell the whiskey
on his breath, but I don't think he really fooled her. Want me to check
the outhouse?"

"Why not? Also, look in the barn. If there is a bottle, it could be
anywhere."

"I really wouldn't bother," said Jenkins.

"Even religious people want to relieve terrible pain," Seth responded,
"and I'm all but certain they wouldn't stock morphine here. That's
what we really need—morphine."

Seth sat at the kitchen table and watched as Possum wolfed down
the ham. "Not bad, is it boy?"

"No sir, not bad at all."

"You rebs don't eat much, do you. Least that's what we hear over in
our lines."

"We were doin' right poorly until we got into Pennsylvania. Then
we started living off your land like you men been living offen ours.
But I ain't had ham for Lord knows how long. Did have some chicken
and a little beef, though. Day before yesterday."

Spenser woke up and looked at the wound in his leg. "God Almighty,
that's looking bad. And it isn't smelling too good either. I need a surgeon,
and that's for certain." He turned toward Seth and Jenkins. "Say, could
you bring me a drink of water, and maybe some in a dish and a cloth so
I could at least cool off this mess."

"I'm still weak, but I'll try to get over to you. Jenkins, how about you?"

"Well, I'd like to help, but my knee is hurtin' pretty bad, too. Maybe we should wait for Kinkaid."

"I can wait."

"I'll use the chair as support. I got along pretty well this morning with it. But I'll have to bring the cup and the dish separately. What do you want to do first, drink or wash?"

"I can do more about my thirst than I can the leg, I guess."

Seth poured water into a cup and, using the chair, walked six-legged over to Spenser. He looked down at Spenser's leg and let out a low whistle. "That is bad, my friend, real bad. I'm no doctor, but I doubt your leg is supposed to look a kind of purple-green . I was at the hospital behind the lines after Chancellorsville, and I saw enough rotten limbs to last me a lifetime here and for eternity. The leg below the knee is going to have to come off."

"I agree — Seth, right? — but where are we going to find a surgeon? They're going to be mighty busy on both sides after all the fighting we've been listening to since earlier this afternoon."

"Well, I don't know. Perhaps we could risk carrying you to some field hospital. Probably a reb one, since we're still in their lines I presume."

"And who's going to do the carrying? Kinkaid is the only one who can move more than six feet without help."

"That's right, of course. Sorry. Well, let's think on it later. Now, I'll do my crab walk or whatever back to the table and get you that dish of water."

Seth came back with the dish of water and a cloth.

"How's your chest? I wondered because of you being weak and all."

"I'm just not able to breathe all that well. I feel as though I'm breathing with one lung. Damn thing hurts, too. We're some group of fighting men, aren't we. If Possum over there had come in with the intention of bagging the whole lot of us, he wouldn't have needed a weapon. Except for the sharpshooter, of course."

"How's our buddy Zinger doing? He seems unusually quiet. Did he go and die on us?"

"No, I told him to shut up and he tried to get out of the chair—I think to attack me—but wrenched his back again and has sat there ever since not saying a word."

"I'm not particularly anxious to help the obnoxious bastard, but I really think he'd be better off lying on the floor than sitting in that rocking chair. That's how he was in the beginning, you know, flat on his back. I think his back gave him the most trouble when he insisted on getting into that rocking chair and standing guard day and night."

Kinkaid exploded into the house. "Guess what?"

"You found some whiskey."

"Not exactly. Here." He handed Seth a jug. "I'm pretty sure this stuff is fermented apple cider. Pretty strong, too."

"How do you know?"

"I tasted it. I had some pretty good swallows, actually. I ain't no boy like this here reb, ya know."

"Let me try it." Seth took the jug from Kinkaid and took a hefty swig. "Say, this isn't bad, and it's strong enough to maybe give Zinger some relief." Kinkaid went to sit down. "One other thing, Davey. Spenser and I think Zinger would be more comfortable lying on the floor. You know, a flat surface that has no give—and doesn't rock."

"So?"

"We need your help to talk him into getting off the chair, first, and then to ease him down."

"He called me a coward, don't forget. That weren't fair. I swore I wouldn't talk to him—ever."

"Ever can mean a long time in some people's lives, Davey, but in a war, ever can be measured in days, hours—even minutes. For you and Zinger, ever is over. Who knows what's going to happen to any of us. A shell or two or three could burst through the roof above and kill all of us instantly. Spenser's leg could... Well, never mind. Davey, we need your help."

"All right, seein' as you put it that way. But I ain't happy about it."

"Neither am I, son."

Seth and Kinkaid took the jug to Zinger. "This is as good as whiskey,

Zinger."

"Shit, apple jack ain't no substitute for whiskey."

"It's all we have, Zinger. Take it or leave it."

"Hand it over. I guess it's better than nothin'." He took the jug from Seth and proceeded to nearly drain it in one long, noisy gulp. "It ain't bad. I'll say that much."

"Zinger, we have a suggestion to make while you're feeling good."

"Who the hell said I was feelin' good. That goddamned stuff ain't even taken hold yet."

"We think you'd be better off lying on the floor instead of sitting in that chair. It isn't helping your back."

"I guess I'm the judge of that. I ain't no good lyin' on the floor, for chrissakes. How can I guard the fuckin' door?"

"Will you please stop that blaspheming!" It was Jenkins, and he was red in the face.

"If you don't like it, Jenkins, stuff your thumbs in your ears." Zinger laughed. Kinkaid joined in and then abruptly stopped because he didn't want Zinger to think he had forgiven him for his earlier condemnation.

"Can we help you down?" Seth asked Zinger.

"I ain't going nowhere, New Yorker. My post is here."

"Why do you want to endure the pain if it can be relieved by lying on the floor?"

Zinger turned in the chair to confront Seth directly, then suddenly arched his back as the pain pushed aside the hard cider. "Oh, oh. For God's sake, do something or put me out of my misery."

"We're trying to do somethin' for ya," said Kinkaid, "but you keep fightin' us."

"Zinger, if you're not any better on the floor, we'll help you back to the chair. Is that a deal?"

Zinger's eyes were closed and he was breathing heavily. "Okay, okay. I'll try the floor, but I want my gun with me. And if I don't like, you men have to get me back here. When I say so."

"Stop giving orders Zinger. You're in no position to do so. Now, see if you can stand."

Holding on to the arms of the chair, Zinger very slowly and painfully raised himself off the seat and finally to an upright position. Seth stood on one side of Zinger and Kinkaid on the other, but his face was turned away from Zinger.

"We're going to lay you down right next to Possum, which is almost in front of the door. See, you'll still be on guard so to speak."

"My lyin' next to a reb and both of us still alive. That wouldn't have happened on the battlefield, I can tell ya."

"You forget, yank. You did kill me, remember?"

"Hell, you ain't dead, boy."

"Might as well be. I ain't no good to nobody now. Not for soldierin', farmin' or courtin'. So, tell me, yank, is that livin'?"

Zinger didn't respond, because at that moment Kinkaid and Seth were lowering him to the floor—slowly, but none too gently. Kinkaid had to do most of the work and he thoroughly relished the fact that his antagonist, at least for a short while, was completely at his mercy. Zinger's string of oaths brought more complaints from Jenkins. Finally, the old man put his hands over his ears and began singing the "Battle Hymn" loudly and off key: "Mine eyes have seen the glory of the coming of the Lord; He is trampling out the vintage where the grapes of wrath are stored..."

Spenser cupped *his* hands over his ears.

The one large room that served the farm family who lately vacated the house as parlor, dining room and kitchen now resembled a hospital ward. The bedding from upstairs that Seth and Spenser used when they lay down was arranged in front of the fireplace at the east end of the room; the armchair Spenser sat in was at the foot of his mattress and close to the front door. The sofa on which Jenkins reclined was against the south wall opposite the front door, and Zinger and Possum were side by side flat on their back between the sofa and front door, with their feet facing the door. Seth had placed a pillow and a rolled up blanket under Zinger's head, even though it put additional strain on his back, because he had insisted on being able not only to see the front door but able to whip his revolver into position quickly. Able-bodied Kinkaid moved about, but much of the time he sat on the floor with his back against the south wall to Jenkins' left, between a side table and a window.

Conversation had ceased for the time being. Spenser and Possum drifted in and out of sleep, the one imagining himself sitting at the typewriter in his closet-like office in Bath knocking out an editorial that concluded, "…and after all the killing, are we any closer to peace?", and the other still dreaming about a summer's day on the bank of the Salkehatchie, but now afraid his feet would no longer feel the cool water let alone carry the sensation to his brain. Jenkins rested his head on an arm of the sofa, trying to ignore the pain in his knee and the occasional pangs that surged up his left arm and lay on his heart like a cannon ball. He read for the third time Psalm 124 in the family Bible: "If it had not been the Lord who was on our side, when men rose up against us, then they had swallowed us up quick. When their wrath was kindled against us, then the waters had overwhelmed us, the stream had gone over our soul. Blessed be the Lord, who hath not given us as a prey to their teeth. Our soul is escaped as a bird out of the snare of the fowlers; the snare is broken, and we are escaped."

Seth sat at the table, elbows firmly planted and hands cupping his head. His brain and heart were elsewhere.

Dearest Goose: I'm all right; at least I think I'll live. Live for you —for us. No one has treated my wounds. I can see the ugly hole in my chest, but of course I don't know what my back looks like where the bullet came out. I guessed I should somehow plug the hole in my chest, but I couldn't find anything here that would do, so I tore a piece of a page from a book, soaked it pretty good in saliva and stuffed it as best I could into the wound. I think it makes me breathe a little easier, but I'm not really sure. It still hurts. I'm sending you a mental picture, but I wonder if you'll ever get it. I don't know much about such things — I mean whether two minds can really meet in space. I guess I have to believe it can happen — like trusting in angels and God Almighty. Anyhow, here goes. There's six of us in this house behind the Confederate line. The most seriously hurt among us yankees is a man from Maine named Spenser; he's probably going to lose his leg. He's usually smoking his pipe, but right now, as you can see, he's nodding off. I like him. A young boy from Philadelphia — the one sitting over by the window staring at nothing in particular — is not wounded, at least not in body. He's got soul scars — like all of us, but maybe more than most. We have a reb here — a real young one — who's paralyzed from the waist down it appears. He surprised us in the house and was shot by one of our men. One of our men! Sorry to say he is. You can see the two of them there on the floor — killer and killed, so to speak. Finally, the old man with his nose in the Bible — course he's younger than our fathers — he's from Michigan. Our spiritual leader you might say. That's everybody. Well, can you see me? Here, at the table? I'm a sorry sight, I'm sure. If you walked through the door this minute and saw me — and smelled me — would you — could you — still love me? Don't answer. Anyway, I still love you. God, I miss you.

The more he thought about it, the more Seth guessed that mental pictures and messages might travel through some kinds of channels in space much like dots and dashes pass along wires between Point A and Point B. He visualized his description of the men in the room pulsating out through his eyes — dit, dit...dot, dot — then soaring high above the house and whatever battlefield carnage had resulted from this day's killing, and tunneling swiftly on fierce, ethereal winds northeast toward Walden. There, above the Vandergosts' gabled and sandstone Dutch house, the mental picture descends — perhaps going down the chimney, unless Mrs. Vandergost was using the fireplace to cook the evening meal —and finally coming to rest in Goose's head as she sits on a chair perhaps shucking corn or churning milk into butter. Maybe she has just taken a peach pie out of the oven and it rests there on the table steaming and filling the room with such a fragrance. Dear God in Heaven, I can smell that pie; I can see it all!

Dearest Yank: If you could only see me now. It's about four o'clock here on the day before the Fourth — one of the hottest days in the last couple of weeks — but I'm in a tub of cool water sipping fresh lemonade. Oh, my goodness, you shouldn't see me now! With no clothes on? Not yet, darling. Of course, my ruffles haven't held back your flourishes before, have they? Tomorrow, the family is going to join with the Bogerts and Sloats for a picnic down along the Wallkill, close to where you and some of your friends used to go swimming. I hate to tantalize you when, God knows, you are living so desperately and meagerly, but I've baked your favorite peach pie, and mother has come up with an apple and a blueberry pie. All for tomorrow's picnic. They're laid out on the table downstairs. I'm sorry, darling. Now, get your mind off the pies and back on me. Oops! Instead of imagining me in the tub, Yank, see me as I'll look tomorrow at the fireworks. I'm going to wear that dark green skirt you like so well, although you kid me about resembling a giant clump of grass when I wear it. We're all thinking of you and saying a prayer for you and all the Orange Blossoms. I sometimes see you in my dreams, all clean and handsome in your new uniform, standing in the ranks while all of Orange County's bigwigs and windbags sent you and your regiment off to war with flags flying. You were so excited, so eager, but, I confess, my heart was doing flip-flops — up for patriotism, down with the dread that something might happen to you, God forbid. Well, Seth, I'm about to climb out of the tub. Close your eyes!

Kinkaid was the first to hear the whooping and hollering followed by the crack of musketry. And it was loud, and it wasn't coming from the north. In fact, as Kinkaid soon discovered looking out the back window near where he had been sitting, a new battle raged not far from the house. "God almighty, it's a cavalry charge! Cavalry! And they're comin' out of the woods near the base of that big round top."

"Whose cavalry?" Zinger was awake, holding his cocked revolver with both hands.

"Ours."

"Who are they charging?"

"The rebels, of course."

"Rebel cavalry?"

"No, infantry."

"Dumb bastards. No cavalry ever made a dent in a solid mass of infantry."

"Oh God, it's awful! Oh sweet Jesus!"

"What's awful? What?" Seth had reached Kinkaid's side.

"Those damn johnnies are cutting down the cavalry as though they was in some kind of shooting gallery. Get outta there boys! Go back to our lines!"

As Kinkaid and Seth watched, the union cavalry — what was left of them — went round and round in circles trying to break out of the ring of fire created by the Confederates. At last they found an opening and skedaddled back into the woods.

Seth turned into the room. "I've never seen anything like it. Not only were they stupid to go up against massed infantry, but the ground is no damned good for a cavalry charge. You can see it out the window. Boulders all over the place. Zinger's right — for a change — poor dumb bastards."

"The dumbest of all are the officers who ordered the charge," said Zinger. His eyes glared especially dark under bushy, black eyebrows. "They ought to hang the whole bunch by their testicles."

Spenser lit his pipe. "An excellent suggestion, my death-dealing and death-defying comrade in arms. What would you say to stringing up all the generals on both sides and, while we're at it, hoisting that ass Buchanan and the politicians and secessionist hotheads who allowed the nation to drift aimlessly into this war — this brutal, unending, senseless civil war?"

"Hold on, Spenser." It was Jenkins, sitting on the edge of the sofa, Bible in hand. "Don't forget, this is a holy war against slavery, the most evil of institutions."

"Holy? How can war be holy?"

"I guess you don't know your Old Testament, comrade. Let me read to you just a few verses from...."

"Never mind."

Jenkins pretended not to hear, and he opened the Bible to First Samuel. "'Then said David to the Philistine, thou comest to me with a sword, and with a spear, and with a shield; but I come to thee in the name of the Lord of hosts, the God of the armies of Israel, whom thou hast defied. This day will the Lord deliver thee into mine hand, and I will smite thee and take thine head from thee, and I will give the carcasses of the host of the Philistines this day unto the fowls of the air and to all the wild beasts of the earth, that all the earth may know that there is a God in Israel.'" Jenkins looked up. "It is the slaveholders, Spenser, who brought on this war, and they and those they send into battle for them must now feel the wrath of a vengeful God. They must know that there is a God in the United States of America."

CHAPTER FIVE
Private Lionel "Zinger" Zook

The blazing sun more deeply reddened, so the survivors thought, because it reflected the blood of 43,000 Americans killed or wounded since July 1, mercifully set at last behind the western mountains. But the humid air hung on to the battle smoke from the day's carnage and would not let it go. Thus, the nostrils of every man still living smarted and their eyes dribbled tears.

In the small house at the southern tip of the great battlefield, Seth and Kinkaid prepared the evening meal of more ham and coffee. What was left of the apple jack was passed from man to man, except Zinger, in whom the alcohol had not only helped to relieve pain, but had caused him to be especially boisterous and blasphemous.

Only Jenkins said grace, and to himself. The others were sure, however, that the old man entreated God to cause the slap-happy sharpshooter to pass out as quickly as possible.

Spenser ate little. He was in considerable discomfort. His leg wound looked worse; the ugly color of infection and decay had begun to spread beyond the gash. He said he was experiencing chills and Seth surmised he was running a fever.

Occasionally, Possum, who rarely spoke unless addressed, twitched uncontrollably, which scared everyone, particularly his floor mate who answered each twitch with his own body jerk, causing him to scream in pain.

Jenkins had asked Seth to find paper and pencil so he could compose some kind of ceremony for the morning—Independence Day. With the Bible at his side, he sat writing and talking to himself: "The word which came to Jeremiah from the Lord, saying, 'At what instant I shall speak concerning a nation and concerning a kingdom, to pluck up, and to pull down, and to destroy it; if that nation, against whom I have pronounced, turn from their evil, I will repent of the evil that I thought to do unto them. And at what instant I shall speak concerning a nation, and concerning a kingdom, to build and to plant it; if it do evil in my sight, that it obey not my voice, then I will repent of the good, wherewith I said I would benefit them'."

After supper, Kinkaid produced a deck of cards he said he had been carrying with him since Fredericksburg. "Adams? Sergeant ? Spenser? Poker or faro?"

All declined, so he arranged the cards for solitaire. Jenkins lay down on the sofa, Spenser was helped to his mattress, and Seth made it to his, with Kinkaid's help. Possum and Zinger on the floor rested their heads on pillows. When Kinkaid had tired of solitaire, he lay down on the carpet at the foot of the bedding on which Spenser slept fitfully and Seth dozed.

The house was quiet, but if the occupants had strained to listen, they would have heard an awful chorus of moans rising to heaven or descending to hell from thousands of broken and bleeding men, some of whom still lay where they had fallen, and many others lying in concentric circles around the field hospitals where overworked and overtired surgeons sawed away smashed arms and legs.

When Zinger was a child, his mother tucked him into bed after prayer on bended knee and whispered, "Sweet dreams, Lionel." This night, his fermented dreams were anything but sweet.

The nightmare began grandly.

He and four of his comrades were parading down Pennsylvania Avenue in Washington, but not on foot in Federal blue. They were astride great white stallions in full medieval armor, lances pointing to the sky. The sound of the hoof beats on cobblestones and the clanking of their suits of mail resounded off the buildings lining the wide boulevard.

Suddenly, from the numbered streets feeding into the avenue came hundreds of maidens swishing their dresses of every rainbow color. Down Thirteenth, Fourteenth and Fifteenth Streets they poured, carrying fragrant flowers in large baskets that they strew in the path of the knights. The girls' still-ripening breasts bobbed just below the heart-shaped neckline of their dress.

"Hail to thee, Sir Lionel," they shouted, and he yelled back, "Don't call me that; it's just Zinger." But they paid no attention, especially after his mother, who inexplicably was sitting on the edge of the roof over the Willard Hotel, raised her voice above all others, "He must be called Lionel; he's my boy, my only son."

Up ahead, Sir Lionel thought he saw a reviewing stand, but as the five horsemen neared the spot, he saw that the bedecked platform held not the President nor his top generals and ministers, but four cannon, each manned by mummies swathed head to foot in Confederate stars and bars. Without commands, the mummies fired their guns.

The missiles approached in slow motion and it was possible for Sir Lionel to see, as they revolved in the air, that each ball was painted a different color and each bore the name of one of the four comrades at his side: George Hodges, Amos Grove, Morris Bream and Lawton Cornwallis—all of whom had been killed during the first skirmish with the Alabamians the day before.

Still moving no faster than spent bowling balls, but on separate tracks, the shells tore off the helmeted heads of his friends. The heads made a terrible racket as they bounced down the avenue, but eventually they were caught by maidens who picked them up and stuffed them into their now-empty baskets.

Sir Lionel put the spurs to his horse and the beast raced forward at such great speed that Foggy Bottom and Georgetown were blurred as he went by. The charger headed not for a bridge, but stretching its legs so that they were almost parallel to the ground, it soared into the air and spanned the Potomac in graceful flight.

The steed landed not across from Washington in Arlington, but at the gates of a fortress, where the battle flags of Confederate regiments drooped listlessly on the ramparts. Iron gates opened without fanfare and Sir Lionel entered, his lance at the ready in the event he had to joust with enemy knights.

There were none.

Instead, horse and rider paraded down a boulevard lined with silent women, some with babies in their arms, some elderly and supported by canes. All wore white dresses, each stained with blood.

In the distance, Sir Lionel could make out a great white house. As he drew nearer, he could see a giant standing on the steps dressed in a white robe, a flowing white beard almost obscuring his face. He halted in front of this king, this god, and as he did so, he sensed that the women who had watched him pass had now converged behind him. They were still silent.

The giant opened his mouth as if to speak, but a flame spewed forth as if from a dragon. It melted Sir Lionel's lance and armor, which fell off him in silvery drops. He stood naked and defenseless.

"Prostrate yourself before the judge," the giant roared, and Sir Lionel lay flat against the ground, trembling. "You are charged with love of killing and other crimes and must now face your accusers."

Lionel raised his head slowly off the ground. Where the giant had been now stood a cross, but it resembled less the cross of Jesus and more the cross hairs of a gun sight. Jefferson "Possum" McCall hung on the cross, his arms draped over the horizontal beam. His legs dangled loose and danced the jig of a marionette whose master has lost control of the strings. The movement was frightening and disconcerting.

"As to the first charge, you are accused of killing dozens of men and boys and taking pride in your accomplishments." Possum's voice was no longer that of a boy, but rather a grown man who had power and knew how to wield it. "How do you plead?"

"Not guilty, of course. I was a knight in the army of my Lord Abraham and obeyed his commands."

"I call Private Eldred Spenser."

Spenser was carried in on a stretcher by four faceless soldiers dressed in Federal blue jacket and Confederate butternut trousers. "Sir Lionel boasted on many occasions of personally killing enemy soldiers. He took pride in the nickname Zinger because it reminded him of how he would carefully and eagerly sight individual Confederate soldiers and then shoot them down as though they were practice targets on the range. The rest of us fired as part of a battle line and we were concerned less with killing the enemy and more with protecting ourselves and our friends from being killed."

"What is your response to the witness, Sir Lionel?"

"I was a sharpshooter, and my job was to pick off individual rebels, especially officers on horseback. I happened to be very good at what I was trained and ordered to do."

"Why, Sir Lionel, did you shoot a defenseless boy, thus paralyzing him from the waist down?" asked Possum without referring to himself directly.

"I was defending my comrades."

"But who among the enemy would have done harm to weaponless, wounded soldiers?"

"The rebs may have captured us."

"And if they had, wouldn't they have attended to you and your comrades' wounds?"

"That's not certain. Anyway, we could have rotted in a rebel prison. Your honor Possum, I already apologized to the boy—to you—for firing the shot that resulted in paralysis."

"Not so, Sir Lionel. You never said you were sorry. Do you now ask forgiveness from the one whose life you have destroyed without just cause?"

"Well, I am sorry you were a boy and not a man."

"You mean you would have shot to kill a man who came to you without a weapon or malice?"

"Well, I suppose…I was defending myself and…"

Possum looked beyond Sir Lionel to the gathered women in their bloody dresses. "As to the charge of loving to kill, how do you find the defendant, guilty or not guilty?"

"Guilty!" they shouted.

"Now, Sir Lionel, your mother and Sergeant Horace Jenkins have charged you with excessive blasphemy. How do you plead?"

"No plea, your honor Possum. I don't know any better."

"That's a lie, your honor." Mrs. Zook was sitting on a cloud that suddenly blossomed. "I taught him to love God and pray daily. I would wash his mouth out with soap or take a switch to him if he used the Lord's name in vain. And that's the truth."

Jenkins limped into view, Bible in hand. "He took extreme pleasure in blaspheming, especially if any God-fearing person such as myself asked him to desist. No sentence you and the women might render could compare to God's judgment. Sir Lionel is destined for hell. And the sooner the better. Amen."

"As to the charge of wanton blasphemy, how do you find?"

Again the women chorused, "Guilty!"

"The final charge is extreme and pitiless meanness. I first call one Davey Kinkaid."

Kinkaid was escorted by an honor guard. Pinned to his new uniform was an oversized medal of honor. "Your honor Possum, this man caused me great anguish when he called me a coward in front of my fellow soldiers. As your honor Possum can plainly see, I have distinguished myself in battle and have been awarded my country's highest honor for valor under fire."

"What do you say to the charge, Sir Lionel?"

"He's lying, your honor. Not only is he not a hero, but he admitted he has never fired a shot in battle."

"Must you shoot, maim and kill in order to be called a hero?"

"I'm not sure. I didn't make the rules."

"Did you call this man a coward?"

"Yes."

"Do you think now you were justified in accusing him of cowardice? You hardly knew this young man at the time, isn't that true?"

"I might have been a little quick to judge."

"There is one more witness. I call your father, David Zook."

Immediately, the face of his dead father filled the screen of his nightmare. Sir Lionel covered his face with his arms as he lay on the ground. His body trembled.

"Lionel, my boy." The voice was soft. There was no anger in it, only sadness. "I regret very much having to return from my grave to testify against you, son. But Lionel—and your honor—the charge is unfortunately correct. I loved my boy. One day I made a mistake and apologized, but Lionel would not accept my apology. Worse, thereafter he would not accept my love. He would not acknowledge my existence. His extreme meanness extended to the day I died when he refused to attend my funeral. Even the angels on high cried for me."

"What do you have to say to this witness, Sir Lionel?"

Sir Lionel lifted his face and it was stained with mud where tears and dust had mixed. "Papa, papa. I was wrong. I know that now. In truth, I knew it all those years when I wouldn't look at you, speak to you or love you. But I would never admit it. I made myself believe that my meanness was justified. Now, papa, please accept my apol…please for…I'm trying to…"

Possum interrupted. "Mother of God, you still can't get the words out of your mouth because they are still trapped in your soul—if they were ever there. You cannot apologize and cannot seek forgiveness because you can't accept it." He turned to the women. "How do you find this defendant, this mean and blasphemous man who delights in killing others?"

The women shrieked their judgement.

"And how do you say he should be punished?"

One of the women, who wore the names of her four dead Confederate sons pinned to the blood splotches on her dress, addressed his honor. " We condemn him to perpetual zinging."

"Then I order you to carry out the sentence."

Sir Lionel raised up off the ground and turned his head to see that the women had raised their arms into a throwing position. In their hands they held long darts.

"Now," said their leader. Each woman shouted "Zing!" and flung her dart at Sir Lionel's bare back. The sharp points plunged in and the pain was unbearable. But he could not cry out. His mouth was open wide, but he could not utter a sound.

He looked up at Possum to plead for his life or his death, but Possum was gone and the giant had returned. He laughed hugely. "Zinging forever. These women will be replaced by others who will in turn be replaced and so on throughout your life. There is no escape from the darts. You will writhe in pain forever."

"No, no. Please, don't make me suffer. Please, please." Sir Lionel crawled on his belly to escape from the women, but they and their darts followed. And they continued to chant, "Zing, zing, zing, zing."

Zinger's eyes popped open.

He was lying on his stomach, breathing hard and perspiring profusely. The pain in his back was excruciating and his head throbbed from earlier overindulgence in apple jack. It took all his will power to swallow screams that swelled up in his throat.

It wasn't that he cared so much for his comrades and the rebel boy next to him that he was afraid he might disturb their sleep. He had never considered how his actions and words might hurt or offend others. But he was fearful that if his house mates were startled by his screams, they might ask questions and he just might, given his present condition and frame of mind, blurt out some details of his nightmare.

He did not need their laughter, their scorn and, worst of all, their agreement with the judgment of his honor Possum and the bloody women.

I can't—I won't lie here any longer, Zinger decided. *I don't know exactly what to do, but I've got to get out of this place somehow, breathe fresh air, maybe clear my head—soak it in a stream.* Unconsciously, he also felt compelled to distance himself from the dream—to somehow outrun the darts.

He grabbed his revolver and crawled ever so slowly and painfully toward the door. Holding on to the knob, he pulled himself up to a crouching position. He thought he would break his spine in two if he attempted to straighten all the way. He opened the door and took the first step since he had first hurt his back. The shooting pain almost caused him to black out.

Outside, he saw the branch Seth had used the day before lying on the ground. He could not bend normally to pick it up, but instead crumpled forward slowly to his hands and knees. He grabbed the branch and used it to raise himself again until he resembled the hunchback of Notre Dame.

Zinger sucked in the air still putrid from the day's battle. He had no idea where he was. He had been carried and dragged to the house by comrades when his back went out and he was unaware of what direction he had come from. Besides, in the dark, shattered trees, boulders and busted farm fences surrounded him on all sides. A branch straight ahead whose leaves had been shredded by minie balls might beckon either to Union or Confederate lines.

"Zing, zing, zing." He could not silence the cries of the bloody women, and the giant still roared "forever" no matter how Zinger tried to shut him out of his consciousness. He stumbled forward, sometimes veering first to the right and then to the left like a crippled drunk.

It was a mistake leaving the house, Zinger concluded. *I did not escape my nightmare and the air burns my lungs rather than refreshing them.* He entered a dense thicket and was totally confused. He stood still lest he trip over roots or fallen limbs—perhaps even a body—and fall down, never to rise again.

As a sharpshooter, Zinger often had been in advance positions as a skirmisher and had then retreated to the main line as enemy pressure and fire increased, and all those times he had never panicked. Thus, the feeling that now invaded his brain and heart and stomach—and every other organ and nerve ending in his body—surprised and frightened him.

"Hey," he yelled out loud, but only ghosts responded.

First, his father emerged from behind a tree and cried, "Why were you so cruel to me, son?" His mother called out from behind, "Lionel, I taught you to pray, remember? Pray now, boy; it's your only hope."

"But ma, I forgot how to pray. I don't know what to say or how to say it. I can't even get down on my knees. I'm frozen in place."

"God wouldn't hear you anyway," volunteered Horace Jenkins, whose voice lay in the leaves or perhaps escaped from some animal's lair in a tree stump. "You used the name of God in vain. You are already condemned to hell."

"Shut up all of you. I've got to think."

"Zing, zing, zing."

"Quiet, you goddamned women."

"Forever, forever. The pain will last forever. There is no escape." The giant's laugh bounced off the trees. It was all around him. And then the trees themselves joined in.

Zinger tried to run, but tripped and tumbled to the ground. In agony, he groped for his revolver.

A shot was heard in the night by a small party of rebels searching for water. And the sound caused three yankees sitting around a dying fire to jerk their heads and cup their ears. Possum stirred fitfully at the report, turned his head slightly and, through sleepy eyes, saw that he was alone on the floor.

CHAPTER SIX
Sergeant Horace Jenkins

Saturday, July 4, was saturated at birth. The humidity clung to everything and everyone. Seth and Spenser, when they awoke, found they and their absent hosts' bedding were equally damp. Jenkins had added great sweat stains to the blood splotches that already discolored the sofa on which he lay cramped, the sofa not being quite long enough to allow him to stretch full length. The wet blanket of still foul-smelling air draped a little less heavy on Kinkaid and Possum sleeping on the floor.

It was Jenkins who first noticed that Zinger was missing. He stirred before the others because he had decided it was his particular duty to ensure that these loyal Americans celebrated Independence Day. He had been preparing a program of sorts since yesterday.

"Where's the blasphemer?" he shouted, not that he missed Zinger.

Possum turned his head. "Don't know, but I kinda think he left some time ago. I remember waking in the dark and not seein' him lyin' there."

"How in the world did he make it out of here? He couldn't hardly crawl let alone walk. And why?"

"Maybe to find some of my friends to kill."

"Now, boy, Zinger was a sinner of the first order, but I don't think he is a cold-blooded killer. No, something else must have taken him outside. But what I wonder?"

Seth heard the two men talking and got up slowly. The weight upon

83

his chest had grown heavier, and each day's breathing had become more painful. Spenser was still asleep, but he exhaled low moans. His leg looked more swollen and discolored. *We've got to get him to a surgeon,* Seth thought.

"Good morning, men."

"It's the Fourth of July, Adams," Jenkins said. "A truly noble day. A day to celebrate."

"I'm not sure any of us feel too much like celebrating, Jenkins."

"Well, I do. In my family—in my part of Michigan, which is flatter than that table there— Independence Day is a whole lot of eating and noise. I recall growing up and picnicking every Fourth of July along the Portage River. We had a spread of beef, turkey and fish from the river; each family brought a different salad; the women baked several varieties of cakes and pies; and, of course, we had ice cream later when the fireworks started and every church rang its bell and every fire station banged out its alarm. It was a belly buster day for certain."

"I don't think any of that's going to happen here today. Besides, the nation is torn asunder. For all we know, the southerners may have won yesterday's battle and America is divided forever."

"No sir, that just could not be. God Almighty won't let it happen. He knows who's in the right and why we're right."

"Maybe, maybe. Say, what's happened to Zinger. Where the hell is he?"

"That's what we've been trying to figure. Possum here says he noticed him missing during the night."

"How did he go? Why did he go? Did he say anything to you, Possum?"

"He was gone when I awoke, remember?"

"Kinkaid!" Seth called for the only able-bodied man in the house.

"He went to the outhouse."

"Maybe Zinger's there, too, although he used the chamber pot before."

Kinkaid entered. "God, ain't it awful today. Can't hardly breathe."

"Davey, Zinger's gone."

"Where could he go, with his back all messed up so's he couldn't

84

hardly sit, stand or lie down?"

"That's what we're all wondering. Maybe you could go out front and look around a little. He couldn't have gone far."

"Iffen you say, but he ain't exactly no friend of mine, y'know. Say, did he take that gun of his?"

Seth looked around on the floor. "He must have. I don't see it."

"I still say he's out hunting my friends," Possum said softly.

"Shut up, Possum." Kinkaid turned on the helpless rebel. "You're our prisoner, y'know."

"I thought you just said he weren't no friend of yours."

"Well, he said some bad things about me, that's for sure, but he's still a comrade. And he ain't no murderer."

"That's what I told him," Jenkins said. "Bad as Zinger is in his soul, he wouldn't kill another human just out of spite or sport. Least I don't think so."

"I'll see if I can find him, but I ain't goin' to take all mornin'. I don't miss him all that much to risk gettin' killed or captured."

"We'll wait on breakfast—if there's going to be any—until you get back," Seth assured Kinkaid as he went out into the early summer haze mixed with yesterday's battle smoke. Seth turned to Jenkins who was sitting on the edge of the sofa holding his knee, which also seemed to be swollen and leaking through the bandage. "So, Jenkins, what do you have planned for us this glorious day in the history of the Union? I could go for either turkey or fish; one salad and one pie would do me just fine. I'll forego the fireworks. I've seen enough of them the last couple of years to last me all the remaining Independence Days of my lifetime."

"Oh, I've got some readings from the Bible, and a few other sayings I've memorized over the years. Then I thought we could share some memories of Independence Days past—like I was doing before—sing a verse or two of the 'Battle Hymn' and close with a prayer for deliverance for the Union and, of course, us."

"How about our boy Confederate here. Possum, do you folks down south still celebrate Independence Day?"

"When I was real little we did some. Old folks said a couple of men from our area had fought in the Revolution—the first one. I don't know if that was true. We was a long ways from the fightin' then."

"How about since this war began—what I presume you think of as a second revolution?"

"No sir. My pa used to say that July 4 was a damn yankee holiday. The north's another country, so we don't celebrate what you do and we don't fly your flag. Least ways that's what pa said."

Jenkins sat up straight. "My boy, whether you like it or not, you are still an American, still a citizen of the United States. You may not fly the flag your ancestors swore allegiance to, Jefferson McCall, but it's still yours. We wait on your eventual return to its fold."

"Well said, Jenkins." Seth leaned over to pat his comrade on the shoulder. "Say, when Kinkaid comes back, maybe he can check to see whether there are any laying hens out back and whether they've done their duty. Also, there must be a cow or…" He caught himself. "Come to think of it, the animals may long ago have been eaten by the rebs. Even by some of our boys."

"We butchered several cows in our regiment alone," Possum volunteered.

"Well, I think there may still be some bread and apple butter. And maybe there's more food down in the cellar that Davey missed before. I expect he got so excited about finding that ham that he forgot to scout for any other edibles."

"We cleaned out a few cellars, too," whispered Possum.

"Let's hope you missed this one. The fact that we found the ham would indicate neither your friends nor my friends plundered this place. Davey can start a fire in the summer kitchen, so we will at least have hot water for coffee. There's still plenty of that."

"Kinkaid? Adams?" Spenser called weakly from his mattress.

"Hold on, Spenser," Seth replied. "Davey is outside, but I'll try to waddle over with my four-legged cane."

Seth finally made it to Spenser's bed. He had propped up two pillows so that he was half sitting. "Adams—Seth—I'm in a bad way. I'm afraid the infection in my leg is going to do me in before long. Someone's got to cut the damn thing off below the knee—and soon."

"I agree, but I don't know how we can get you to a hospital, and I haven't seen anybody come by here in awhile."

"Maybe Kinkaid could be a search party of one to scare up a surgeon. Reb or Union, I don't care."

"The problem is that the rebs might shoot or capture Kinkaid. Then you don't have a surgeon and we have no fit body to do chores and such."

"Is there some kind of saw or butcher knife around here?"

"I suppose… What the hell are you thinking?"

"I'm thinking that maybe you and Kinkaid are going to have to pretend to be surgeons."

"For God's sake, Spenser, we don't know the first thing about amputating a leg. We'd kill you for sure. You'd probably bleed to death before we even finished. Lord, what an idea."

"Please think about it. You may be my only chance. I'd rather die at your hands than die a putrid death here in bed."

Seth changed the subject. "Zinger's gone. Left during the night."

"He's gone? Somebody must have kidnapped him and dragged him out the door. I wonder why he didn't fire his gun at whoever snuck in and snatched him." A thin smile came over his face. "Wait a minute—who the hell would want him?"

"I'm sure nobody took him. Somehow he got out by himself. Davey's out looking for him."

"What is Davey going to do if he finds him, bring him back here? We don't want him either."

"I never thought about what Davey would do if he found Zinger sitting by a tree or fence post, revolver ready. I guess it depends on why Zinger left here in the first place. Possum thinks he went out hunting for rebs."

"Possible, very possible. He's the only soldier I've met in two years who really loved the killing. I feel sorry for the poor bastard. Well, almost."

"Spenser, can you get up at all? Davey will make some coffee and there's plenty of bread and apple butter. Also, Jenkins has his heart set on celebrating Independence Day."

"My God, I forgot this was the Fourth of July. What's to celebrate?"

"For one thing, he wants each of us to reminisce about past celebrations."

"The only way I can get out there is if somebody—you and Kinkaid, I guess—helps me to my chair. I don't want to put pressure on this leg."

"Okay. As soon as Davey returns, we'll come get you."

Seth heard the door open and close, and he shuffled back to the kitchen using the chair. Kinkaid was sitting at the table. His eyes stared without seeing.

Jenkins spoke first. "Well, what did you find out? Did you find Zinger?"

Kinkaid responded without looking at anyone. "He's out there all right, but dead with a bullet hole in his head."

"Do you think he shot it out with some reb skirmishers?" Seth asked.

"Not likely. He had his revolver in his hand, but my guess is he killed hisself. Yessir, put a bullet in his own brain. Don't ask me why."

"Committed suicide? He didn't seem the type. All the bravado and everything."

"It was his way of erasing his sins," Jenkins said.

"I don't buy that, Jenkins. Zinger may have been sinful—you seem to know more about sin than I do—but I doubt he thought of himself that way. Davey, where did you find him?"

"Not far. The body's in some trees just t'other side of the field out front. I still say he killed hisself—and because of his pain. Remember yesterday when he asked me to shoot him so's he wouldn't have to suffer no more. By the way, here's his revolver." He laid it on the table.

"Did you bury him?"

"Hell no. I didn't have no shovel. Besides, I didn't want to stay too long out there. I don't know who's where. I coulda been shot or taken."

"I suppose a burial party will come along eventually and take care of Zinger."

"We ought to consider praying for Zinger's soul," Jenkins said, "although I don't think there's much chance of keeping it from being snatched by the devil."

"First, let's get Spenser out here. Davey, I'll need your help. He'll probably have to make a stop at the commode, too. By the way, has that been emptied?"

"Not by me."

"Why not? You're the only one who can."

"I s'pose so, but I'm gettin' kinda tired of doing all the chores. Can't you do more?"

"I wish I could, but I'm already doing more than my body tells me I should. I get exhausted after the least exertion."

"Okay, okay. Let's get Spenser."

Seth and Kinkaid brought Spenser out to his chair, but the effort caused Seth to sit at the table and wheeze. At last, he stood up and, using his chair as a cane and with assistance of Kinkaid, prepared breakfast of bread and jam. Kinkaid then went to the summer kitchen to heat water for coffee.

After breakfast, Kinkaid went back to the cellar to hunt for more food. He returned with a basket of peaches, half of which had spoiled; green beans and squash. He said he had found no more meat or poultry. And, in a return visit to the barn and other farm buildings, he saw no animals. There was evidence, however, that there had at least been chickens. In one corner of a feed lot, Kinkaid found nearly a dozen chicken heads. Apparently, rebel soldiers had discovered this place before them.

Then it was time for the celebration, for which Jenkins' enthusiasm far surpassed that of the others' combined.

To begin, Jenkins recited from memory a passage from the Declaration of Independence: "'We hold these truths to be self-evident, that all men are created equal, that they are endowed by their creator with certain unalienable rights, that among these are life, liberty and the pursuit of happiness.'" His comrades listened patiently, mopping their brows and brushing away flies, most of which circled Spenser's open wound and Jenkins' bandaged but oozing knee.

Jenkins' blue jacket lay over the back of the sofa, and he slipped his hand into an inside pocket from which he withdrew a folded newspaper article, yellowing and much-stained. He explained that the article came from the Battle Creek Enquirer and was a report of President Lincoln's inaugural address which he had carried with him since leaving home in the summer of '61. He turned to Possum on the floor. "Pay close attention to these words, son:

"'I hold that, in contemplation of universal law and of the Constitution, the union of these states is perpetual. Perpetuity is implied, if not expressed, in the fundamental law of all national governments. It is safe to assert that no government proper ever had a provision in its organic law for its own termination. Continue to execute all the express provisions of our national Constitution and the Union will endure forever—it being impossible to destroy it, except by some action not provided for in the instrument itself.'"

"See Possum, South Carolina is still a part of the Union whether your leaders, family and friends think so or not. The nation cannot be destroyed from within. Now, of course, God can destroy it if he chooses." At this point, Jenkins read the passage from Jeremiah he had copied down yesterday.

"Do you think God is destroying the Union, Jenkins?" You could hear the pain in Spenser's voice.

"No, I don't. I believe, however, he will destroy the southern government. Their so-called confederacy will be trampled down like the 'vintage where the grapes of wrath are stored.'" Possum hummed a few bars from Dixie so softly that no one heard.

"Now," Jenkins waxed, "it's time for remembering great Independence Days past. I've already said my piece." He looked at the others. Let's see." He looked at each one again. "Adams, you start us off."

"I don't know how interesting or entertaining this reminiscing is going to be, but here goes. As you know, I'm from New York State—Walden, a village west of Newburgh, which is a port on the mighty Hudson River above New York City. Most of what occurs in Orange County—my unit's called the Orange Blossoms, by the way—revolves around the river.

"On the Fourth of July there's a parade that begins down by the river and comes up Broadway. Back in 1857 I remember standing along the sidewalk and watching the color guard go by and seeing a veteran of the War of 1812 decked out in his uniform, and his white hair and beard blowin' in the wind. Did he ever get the cheers.

"The parade always winds up at Washington's headquarters on Liberty Street. It's an old Dutch fieldstone house that Washington used for more than a year toward the end of the Revolution. That's where the speeches are made—for most of the afternoon.

"The young people start to drift off after the first round. Some of them head for the river and go swimming or boating. I don't mind telling you some honest to goodness courting went on, too. It was a big time." Seth glanced out the window. "God willing, me and what's left of the Orange Blossoms will march up Broadway when all this is over and done with."

"Fine, fine, Seth. Now, Spenser, how about you?"

Spenser adjusted his outstretched, propped-up leg and winced. He exhaled a long sigh. "I guess I'm farthest from home, with the exception of our southern friend here. In northern Maine, of course, Independence Day can still be a might chilly. Summer is a short season up there among the pines, so there's no swimming and very little boating.

"I guess what I remember best about the Fourth of July is the morning church service and then the picnic lunch in the cemetery. See, Jenkins, you're not the only believer present."

"I never assumed I was, Eldred."

"Well, there was a whole lot of singing of hymns and patriotic songs. Then kind of a strange tableau, with kids taking the part of some of the signers of the Declaration. John Adams was the favorite. The boy playing Washington would speak first and say that the Declaration was complete and ready to be signed. The strange part, but in keeping with the location of this production, was when a boy or girl—it didn't matter much either way to most people—dressed as Jesus would stand up in the balcony at the back of the church and say, 'God bless you men for doing my will in forming this great nation.' Then the signers would go up one by one to a table and record the name of the person they were portraying. Actually, it was kind of moving."

"You had lunch in a cemetery?" Kinkaid asked.

"I guess that sounds strange, but in a way the headstones in a town's cemetery are like pages in its history. Abbreviated, naturally, but nevertheless informative and revealing. I remember one headstone, for example. The name was...wait a minute, I'll remember...a...Augustus Reliance Montpelier...the third. Well, among the things you learned was that Montpelier was a member of the first legislature after Maine broke away from Massachusetts in 1820. His stone also records that he was a founder of the first public school in that part of Maine.

"The cemetery contains the remains of men who fought in the Revolution and the War of 1812, captains and ordinary seamen of early whaling vessels, and women who nursed the community during the various epidemics. I recall one headstone whose epitaph read, 'Here rests'—now, I forget the name— 'who bore the slings and arrows of his friends and neighbors who unjustly accused him of sinful ways'—not specified— 'but who was finally judged to be innocent of all wrongdoing and now has a secure and honorable place in the memory of this community and a just reward in Heaven'.

"Yes, I probably learned as much about my hometown and the people who grew up with it from July Fourth picnics in the cemetery as I did from my history teachers. I guess that's my contribution Jenkins—Horace—and thanks for forcing me to remember those days. Frankly, I thought your idea of celebration was a bad one, considering our present situation as men and as a country, but this has been a good experience. I haven't thought about that Independence Day tableau and the picnics for a long time."

Everyone turned toward Kinkaid, who was now seated on the floor leaning against the wall. Jenkins spoke, "Davey, it's your turn. By the way, whereabouts in Pennsylvania do you hail from?"

"Near Washington's Crossing on the Delaware."

"Tell us a little about that area, will you."

"What's to tell?"

"That's historic ground, isn't it?"

"Well, I reckon. That's where Washington took his army over to New Jersey and the battle at Trenton. A couple of years ago, a bunch of us kinda borrowed a boat out of a shed on the day before Christmas and started to row across through the ice. We had too many in the boat and almost sunk. When we got home, our parents licked us proper." Davey laughed. "Petey Forbush had an icicle hanging from his nose."

"What about Independence Day celebrations?"

"Two years ago, me and my family went into Philadelphia. Started out at dawn and spent the whole day; almost midnight before we got home. Saw the spot in front of Independence Hall where Mr. Lincoln spoke on his way to Washington in the spring.

"The fireworks was the best. I mean they was shootin' rockets over the buildings. And ground displays, they was really somethin'. An American flag took up half a block, all popping and sizzlin'. The heads of Jefferson, Washington and Madison was all white hot, so bright you could read the paper by it. The heads went up to the second story.

"At the end, there were a huge torchlight parade with soldiers and sailors and all manner of folks carrying torches and singing one thing after another. That's when I decided to join up. This sergeant marching by—more'n six feet and eyes blacker than his beard—looked right at me—me being only sixteen at the time—and said, 'Boy, we need you.' That's all he said and went on, but… well, here I am."

"Thank you men." Jenkins looked as proud as a teacher whose students have all recited perfectly. "Possum, do you have anything to say?"

"I don't think so, but y'all have had right interesting stories to tell."

"Suppose we sing a stanza or two of the 'Battle Hymn.'" Kinkaid and Seth stood up, Seth leaning on his chair-cane. "Mine eyes have seen the glory of the coming of the Lord," Jenkins began. The others tried to join in, but Jenkins wandered among the keys and the others became lost following his erratic lead. They finally came together loudly for the refrain and, after only the one verse, stopped singing.

"Join me now in prayer, please." Jenkins paused until every head was bowed. "Almighty and everlasting father, we thank you for your many blessings, especially for this great nation and those who forged it, shaped it according to your design, and who have died to preserve it. Continue to guide the nation's course and bring to an end this terrible war and the institution of slavery that has helped to fuel the flames of division and hatred among fellow Americans. Grant healing to those who have been maimed in the nation's defense. And, yes Lord, we also ask your comfort and healing for those wounded on the other side, who oppose us and call us enemy, but whom we have never stopped loving as brothers in Jesus Christ, in whose name we pray. Amen."

Jenkins' "amen" not only ended the celebration – if one could call it that –but it seemed to silence any further conversation. Each man withdrew into himself, perhaps the natural result of his earlier reminiscing. Seth sat at the table, his head resting on his folded hands.

Dearest Goose: I can imagine you in that green skirt and how it spreads over the ground and blends into the grass where you and your family are picnicking under the trees today. There you are, propped up or laying back with your arms behind your head, the prettiest adornment on that emerald carpet that seems to go on forever in all directions. Maybe toward me. I can picture that green tide flowing south and west, first connecting to New Jersey grass on the other side of the Ramapos, and then somehow skipping over the Delaware River – perhaps carried one clump at a time in a wheelbarrow on a ferry boat, or perhaps clinging to the bark of a downed elm borne by a swift current – and then attaching to Pennsylvania grass. If I dare look out the window now, will I see a lush green wave that began on the bank of the Wallkill River cascading down off the western ridge and blanketing boulders and bloated bodies till it comes to rest against the hollyhocks that lean their blossoms against this house — this hospital? Will I also see you, darling?

Eldred had it right, Seth mused, when he thanked Horace for forcing him to remember good times that seemed much longer ago than the ten or fifteen years since they were children and their families shared a sacred holiday and the states, north and south, still shared a sacred dream first dreamed almost a century ago. Seth reasoned his feelings about Independence Day and his views on the war and his part in it were considerably different from those that guided Eldred and Horace.

Eldred was bitter and resentful, first because politicians and declared patriots both north and south had not prevented war and, in the end, because he felt obliged to submit to the Union's call to arms and then surrender to that most deadly and unarguable cliche – kill or be killed. To Horace, who feared both God's wrath and man's detachment from God, the war was simply God's punishment on those who believed in and practiced slavery, and who, at least, did the bidding of the slaveholders by serving in the armies of the illegitimate Confederate States of America. Both men, while they celebrated Independence Day and paid sincere homage to the nation's founders and original defenders, probably never felt or appreciated America's birth pains as keenly as Seth and others like him who grew up in the cockpit of the Revolution and were reminded almost daily of the sacrifices that saved the weak and vulnerable infant nation from a premature death. For Seth, this war — this Gettysburg battlefield — were extensions – no, continuations – of the Revolution. The Union still had to be saved from its enemies, those who would kill it before it could mature and grow into whatever greatness it was destined to become. *How ironic, how terribly regrettable,* Seth thought, *that Possum, his kinfolk, and presumably most southerners believed that secession and this war constituted a second revolution, and these United States of America that Seth's ancestors, among so many others, had fought to preserve was now, in their mind, the mother country turned father dictator. For them, President Lincoln was King George reincarnated.*

In Seth's corner of the original thirteen colonies, unlike the flat mitten of lower Michigan or the jagged coast of Maine, the Revolution was not just an historical event to be remembered and to rejoice in; it was a lively presence. In church cemeteries within walking distance of Seth's home were headstones of men killed in action downriver at Haarlem Heights, Chatterton's Hill and Fort Washington. He and two friends, when they were in their early teens, scaled the rocks of Stony Point to reenact Mad Anthony Wayne's midnight assault on the British garrison there. The boys whittled long sticks until, in their youthful imagination, they resembled the bayonets used to skewer nearly 150 of His Majesty's regulars, many in various stages of undress.

In the company of his father, Seth had gone down to Tappan, and while his father sipped ale in the tavern where the British spy Major John Andre was tried and convicted, Seth walked up the nearby hill to the place where Andre had been hung. Every child in those parts could recite from memory Andre's last words, "I pray you to bear me witness that I meet my fate like a brave man." They knew that quote even before their teachers made them learn Nathan Hale's gallows speech.

Most of all, until about twenty years ago, the Revolution still lived in the mind and soul of a handful of ancient veterans, who passed down their grand stories of war and peace, most of them embellished through the years . Seth had a vague recollection of sitting at the foot of Cornelius Sloat when the onetime sergeant in New York's Ulster County regiment, who was nearly ninety at the time, recounted his service in short, labored sentences barely audible to the six-year-old Seth. The old man's skin had resembled that of a Hudson River shad rotting on the shore of an inlet at the base of Storm King mountain. His hair, what was left of it, hung in white strings, and his eyes had long ago dimmed behind opaque cataracts.

He told of being captured in the rout of Washington's army on Long Island and imprisoned in the Bowerie in New York City. Seth's child's mind didn't register all that Sloat said, and he had since forgotten even some of the details he once knew, but he would never forget how that wrinkled, gray face leaned over to where Seth sat popeyed and the sergeant of yore whispered, "I escaped from that prison, boy, and then do you know what I did?" Seth, of course, had been speechless. "Why, I rejoined the army. And do you know why I rejoined the army, boy?" He again answered his own question, "Because my new country still needed me."

Seth was the first to notice that Spenser had slumped, his chin resting on his chest. He hurried over as fast as his chair-cane would take him. "Eldred, Eldred!" Spenser did not respond, but he was breathing. Seth felt his forehead and cheeks. They were very hot, but he was not perspiring like everyone else. "Davey, soak a cloth in cold water and bring it to me, please." Kinkaid brought him the cloth and Seth applied it to Spenser's forehead. He roused slightly.

"What's wrong, Seth?" Jenkins asked.

"It's a high fever connected to this wound in his leg, I assume. It looks real bad."

"What should we be doing for him?"

"I don't know. What he needs is a surgeon to take off his leg, but God only knows how or where we could find one. We're not even sure where the lines are anymore."

"Seth?" Spenser's voice was low and weak, and he raised his head only slightly.

"Yes, Eldred." Seth bent down to listen.

"Seth, I have only two options left. Either you cut off this bad leg—now—or I'm going to blow out my brains with Zinger's revolver. Which way is it going to be?"

CHAPTER SEVEN
Private Davey Kinkaid

Some thought it had to do with whatever chemicals were released by the explosion of gunpowder rising up into the sky and somehow combining with or reacting upon vapor in clouds. Others were just as sure the Creator had seen about all the slaughter he could stomach and that he felt it necessary to wash away the aftermath of man's most colossal sin, even if he could not or would not forgive and forget the sin itself. But every man on both sides of the valley of death at Gettysburg knew it was going to rain this July Fourth because it always did the day after a great battle. It began as a fine mist in the early afternoon, but by the time the long trains of wagons carrying the broken and bleeding bodies of Confederate soldiers slogged west toward the Blue Ridge Mountains, the drizzle had become a steady downpour.

Seth and Kinkaid sat at the kitchen table debating whether they should allow Spenser to die slowly from the spreading infection in his leg or take a chance on killing him quickly by botching an amputation.

Jenkins dozed on the sofa and Spenser lay on his mattress, burning up with fever and only semi-conscious. His putrefying leg oozed into the blanket. Possum was awake, staring at the ceiling and brooding deeply about going home as half the boy he was when he left.

Seth spoke to himself as much as to Kinkaid. "Suppose we were to decide to take off Spenser's leg, I guess we could use my large pocket knife for flesh and muscle and maybe a saw for the bone. If we had one."

"I don't know as we oughta try this at all."

"He told me to do it or he'd blow his brains out."

"You don't put no stock in that, do you? Besides, we just keep the gun away from him. That's simple enough."

"Then what, Davey, do we all sit around and watch him slowly suffer and the infection spread and his body swell up and smell up until he dies of decay and the flies cover him like a black blanket? God, I don't think I could be a witness to that."

"So instead we stand around while he bleeds to death."

"No. I mean that doesn't have to happen. I know a little about stopping bleeding. I've seen doctors in the field do it by applying a tourniquet, tying off arteries and packing the wound."

"Sounds like you got your mind all made up."

"I'm talking out loud. You're not helping any."

"What do you want me to say. I don't think we can save him. Besides, I ain't sure I have any stomach for cutting off a leg."

"Stomach? Stomach?! So you puke a couple of times and wet your pants. You still can be of some help. I can't do it by myself, and Jenkins and Possum are hardly up to it. I'm barely up to it myself. I'm not sure I'll be able to stand on *my* legs long enough to get *his* leg off."

"Have you thought where you'd do it—the operating?"

"I remember hearing some stretcher bearers talk about taking men to a house where the surgeon did the cutting on the kitchen table. So, I guess we'll do it right here."

"Where we put out the food?"

"If you have a better idea, I'm open."

"I reckon not."

"Davey, please go to the barn and other buildings to see if you can come up with a small saw. While you're out there, look for a horse blanket or something we can use to cover the table, and— oh yes— another bottle of apple jack would help."

"That's it, then. We're going ahead?"

"I think we have to, Davey. It's our only real choice, the only hope for poor Eldred. Go ahead, now. I'll see to sharpening my knife and

finding something we can use to tie off arteries and pack the stump."
Kinkaid went out the door.

Seth propped his elbows, cupped his head in his hands and stared out the rear window. Through the curtain of rain he could see men moving among the carcasses – man and beast — that littered the boulder-strewn slope where the senseless charge by Union cavalry had been repulsed late yesterday afternoon by some of those same cursed Texans who, two days ago, had shattered and scattered the Orange Blossoms. Some men bore litters; others shouldered shovels.

Dearest Goose: I probably should be praying to God, but I feel closer to you. I've just decided to do something I have no business doing. I'm going to take a man's leg off. Am I a fool? Worse, am I a butcher, a murderer? If I do nothing, maybe Eldred will live long enough for a proper doctor to arrive on the scene and perform the amputation. The fighting must be over – at last – so we're sure to be found sooner or later. But, then, that's the problem, isn't it. Will later be too late for Eldred? I imagine every doctor on both sides has been sawing off arms and legs since July 1, with no end in sight. Many wounded are just now being carried off the field. I've never felt so alone, so disheartened.

If you could only come to me and wrap your arms around me, press your cheek against mine until our tears shed equally over happy reunion and for poor Eldred mixed together just as our very lives are forever inseparable. If you can't come, can at you at least tell me if I'm doing right? Lorranah, I need you. Desperately.

Dearest Yank: A thunderstorm has spoiled our picnic, just as it did the last time you were here to share the day with us. You, a fool, a butcher, a murderer? No, Seth. You may be a so-so farmer and an off-key singer, but you're none of those other things. You said you have no business performing this amputation, but I strongly disagree. For the last year and more you've been engaged in a rotten business thrust upon you. I know how you feel about preserving the Union, and, unfortunately, our nation will be divided – perhaps forever – unless you and your comrades defeat the Confederate army. But, Seth, here's your opportunity to engage in the business of saving life instead of destroying it. My tears I cry for you, darling, and my prayer implores God to direct your hand and to comfort your friend, Eldred. I love you.

"Hey, yank?" Possum broke into Seth's long distance communication.

"Yes?"

"I confess to bein' a might groggy, but I thought I heard y'all talkin' about takin' somebody's leg off. I hope y'all ain't talkin' about me, 'cause I aim to keep my legs – both of them – even though they ain't all that much good to me."

"I think we're going to amputate Spenser's bad leg."

"Oh." There was a long pause. "Do you know how to do that, yank?"

"Not exactly. I've seen some cutting done before. By doctors. But...well...we'll do our best."

Seth rose slowly from his chair and commenced hunting for a whetstone. He found one in the corner cupboard, took it back to the table, sat down and sharpened the four-inch blade of his folding knife. He stood up again, becoming conscious that too much exertion now could jeopardize the operation, but he had to find heavy thread and packing material.

"Packing, packing," he muttered to himself. "What the hell do I use to pack the stump, to help control the bleeding?" He had witnessed, fairly close up, a couple of amputations in a field hospital back in May at Chancellorsville. He had brought in a wounded comrade and, after laying the man down on straw scattered on the ground outside the hospital tent, he stood near the entrance to the tent and watched with gruesome fascination as doctors removed one man's shattered leg and then another soldier's arm. Finally, an orderly yelled at him to get away and he drifted into a nearby woods where he vomited for five minutes.

Seth crab-walked with his chair to the chest of drawers in the front left corner of the room adjacent to the bedding he slept on, which was next to the bedding used by Spenser. He began rummaging through the drawers. In the next to last drawer he came across a bolt of unbleached muslin, perhaps intended for sheets, a fall dress or a man's shirt. He grabbed the cloth and placed it on the seat of the chair he was using for locomotion.

"All right," he mumbled, "I've packing. What I need now is some thread to tie off arteries. I don't know what the surgeons use, but whatever the woman of this house has for sewing and darning will have to do. Now, where would she keep thread?" He pictured his mother sewing. She sat in a chair by a table, facing the fireplace in winter. In warm weather, she moved the chair by a window or door. She kept her thread and needles and such in a basket. "Okay, where did she put the basket when she wasn't using it?" He answered his question, "Alongside the fireplace."

He looked toward the fireplace and there under the window was a basket. It even looked like his mother's. He went over, picked it up and set it on the seat of the chair. He was about to return to the kitchen when it occurred to him that he would also need a tourniquet. Perhaps a man's belt. He remembered seeing one in the chest of drawers. His scavenger hunt ended there, and he returned to the kitchen table with his makeshift medical paraphernalia.

His chest cavity rattled. "My God," he wheezed, "how am I going to make it through an amputation if I can't stand on my feet for more than five or ten minutes? Davey's going to have to help more than he thinks. Maybe he can do the cutting and the sawing and I'll handle the packing. Or vice versa. Maybe I'll get old Jenkins to cut up this muslin. He can certainly do that much."

He decided it might be a blessing that Spenser was semi-delirious with fever, especially if Davey couldn't find any more apple jack. "Lord, Lord," he muttered, "don't let Eldred yell and carry on. I wouldn't be able to continue and he would surely die. Probably will anyway. I'm no surgeon. I'm probably not even strong enough to complete the job. Who knows whether I can prevent him from bleeding to death. I must get Jenkins to say a prayer, a whole string of them. One after another during the operation." He remembered he and Spenser already had one prayer – Lorannah's.

The front door opened and Kinkaid entered. "We're in luck—I guess. The man who owns this place must do some pretty fancy carpentry. He had several saws and I picked this here one." Kinkaid held up a saw that measured twelve to fifteen inches and had small teeth.

"That looks like it'll work, Davey. Thanks."

"And here's the blanket. This musta come off one of our men, 'cause it's got U.S. written right here." He pointed to the official government issue logo. "Somebody musta been in the barn. In fact, I know so. I saw a bloody boot there and stains on the straw. I wonder what happened to whoever was in there. Maybe one of the troopers from yesterday's charge." He paused, then smiled. "I got a surprise, too." Kinkaid slowly turned around to reveal a bulge in his back pocket.

"Whiskey!" Kinkaid and Seth said it together.

"Where did you ever find that flask? You must have missed it before. Poor Zinger must be looking down—or up—and cussing you out for not finding whiskey when he craved it so much."

"No, the flask was by this here blanket. Neither one was there when I went out yesterday. The flask ain't full, o'course, but it'll help. Right?"

"Sure it will, Davey. You did very well. I also found what I was looking for." Seth showed Kinkaid the muslin, thread and belt. His knife was lying beside them. "I'm going to get Jenkins to cut the muslin into large squares that can then be folded."

"Do we need anything else, Seth?" It was the first time the boy had called him by his first name.

"We should have a bucket of water on hand so I can rinse off the knife and saw as necessary, and also to soak some of the packing."

"Okay, I'll get some more water." He grabbed the bucket by the kitchen fireplace and went outside.

"Horace, Horace." Seth, who was sitting at the table, tried to rouse Jenkins. "Horace, I need your help."

The old man stirred and rubbed his eyes. "You say you need me?" He was still lying down.

"Yes. We're—Davey and me—we're going to amputate Eldred's leg. Otherwise, I fear he'll die. He wants me to."

Jenkins sat up with effort. "God Almighty, are you — is Spenser — up to that? Do you know…?"

"Horace, don't bother asking the question. It's already been asked and answered. Amputation is the only course we can take. It's Eldred's only chance."

"I'm not sure I can do much for you. I'm sorry, Seth. This knee is hurting more than ever. I suppose eventually I'll lose my leg, too, but I think I'll wait for a doctor. I'm not as bad off as poor Eldred."

"You don't need to get up. What I have in mind for you is cutting up this muslin into pieces approximately twelve by twelve inches. I need them to pack the stump. All right?"

"Of course. Hand me the material and scissors."

"Shit. Scissors. All right, I'll get them, or Davey will when he comes in. One other thing Horace. Your specialty."

"And what's that may I ask?"

"Prayer. And lots of it. For Eldred, of course, but also for Davey and me. As you implied with your question, we aren't altogether sure of what we're going to do, plus Davey's likely to pass out at the sight of blood, and I'm liable to keel over because my body won't stand up any longer."

"I don't think I'd call praying a specialty, but I'm happy to do it. To myself or out loud?"

"What?"

"Shall I pray quietly or speak out so you can hear what I'm praying."

"Geez, I don't know. I guess start out quietly. If things get rough, which I fully expect, I may call on you at any moment to shout prayers."

Davey came in with the bucket of water. He was drenched. "That rain's coming down something fierce. Just like Chancellorsville. Remember?" .

"Wonderful." Spenser was awake. "Maybe it will wash away the stains from the last whatever days we've been here killing each other."

"Eldred, you won't have to kill yourself."

"That's also good news. You've decided to cut this foul thing off, then?"

"Yes. Whenever you're and we're ready."

"Any time, Seth. The sooner the better."

"After supper," Kinkaid said. "I ain't goin' to be a part of no amputatin' before supper."

"Aren't you afraid that if we wait until after supper you'll throw up our meager provisions all over yourself and maybe the patient and chief doctor?" Seth asked.

"Don't worry. If I spill my guts, I'll aim at the enemy here." He pointed to Possum on the floor.

"Thanks," the boy responded. "When I get away from you yanks, I'll get word to Gen'l Lee to pass the word to all our boys to hunt you down like foxes and give you a right good volley."

"Who says you're going back to your lines. We'll take you to a hospital first and then dump you in a prison up north. Count on it, Reb."

"All right, boys." Jenkins interjected. "Davey, you're not going to vomit on Possum, and Possum, you're not going to turn Davey into a target for the Army of Northern Virginia. The war's over in this house. We're no longer warriors, just war's victims trying to stay alive a little longer and, while we're at it, trying to make friends of enemies."

"Bravo, bravo!" Spenser had pushed up his pillows so that he was half sitting up. He started to laugh. "Poor Zinger would be turning over in his grave— if he was in one."

"Well, Davey, gather up what food we have." Seth remained seated. He needed all his strength for later. "I think there are some peaches, and I suppose we could cut up some of those green beans and squash."

"And more apple butter and bread."

"We're getting low on both, Davey, and God only knows how much longer we'll have to hold out here."

The evening meal — taken in the late afternoon —was a tablespoon of green beans, two of squash and a peach for each man, except Spenser. Seth said he shouldn't have anything on his stomach except whiskey, which would be administered soon.

The men sat in silence as they ate. The only sound was the incessant ping, ping, ping as giant raindrops pounded the roof over their head. Occasionally, the flash of lightning and boom of thunder mocked the roar of cannon. Kinkaid went to the window facing west to watch clouds black as coal scud off the Blue Ridge, now visible as though seen through gauze. Lightning flashed nearby and cast Kinkaid's shadow on a painting of the distant mountains that hung on the rear wall.

"Doctor, can I smoke while I'm waiting for you and young Davey to work your miracle?"

"I suppose. Davey – thank God, your legs work – will you give Spenser his pipe and tobacco."

"Okay, but everyone here owes me for bein' their nigger boy." He took Spenser his pipe and tobacco.

"That word offends me, Davey." Jenkins was sitting up straight, rubbing the pain in his chest.

"What word?"

"The word nigger demeans the people we're sworn to save."

"How's that? I didn't swear to save no slaves."

"As he – Jesus – died to make men holy, let us die to make men free. Don't you remember the words to the 'Battle Hymn'?"

"I never paid all that much attention."

"If I may interrupt." Spenser puffed on his pipe. "When you butchers are through with me, I'd really appreciate your taking me outside and plopping me in the rain, bloody stump and all. It would feel so damned good. Maybe I could imagine myself sitting on this cliff that juts into the ocean a few miles north of my hometown. I used to sit there a lot when I was home from college, especially – if you can believe it – when a storm was starting to boil out to sea. I figured – as only a boy in his teens would dare – that I could stare down old Neptune or God Almighty – whoever it was causing the waves to heave and the wind to shriek. I once wrote about my youthful arrogance in the face of true omnipotence. It was the first thing I had published in the paper. I was nineteen." Spenser blew out a cloud of smoke and stared into space.

"I'll make a deal, Eldred. After the operation, if you're conscious and feel up to it, Davey and I will take you out on the porch and you can watch the rain – but not sit in the mud — and catch whatever breezes are blowing. In fact, we'll make preparations now. Davey, see if you can drag Eldred off his bedding so he can lean against the wall by the fireplace. Then take his bedding out on the porch—the covered part, naturally. How's that sound?"

"I'm going to take that as a promise, Seth."

"Now, I have more good news for you, Eldred."

"More? Aside from going outside to watch the rain, that is if I'm alive and awake—no offense Seth—I don't recall any good news in one hell of a long time."

"Well, whiskey is as good as it's going to get for now."

"Whiskey?"

"Yes, Davey here found two-thirds of a flask out in the barn. And before you say anything, it wasn't there when Zinger was thirsting for a swig. We guess it might have been left by some young officer that was cut down when he and his imbecile comrades rode their horses into Texas hell yesterday afternoon. The whiskey will have to take the place of chloroform or ether."

"All right. I was prepared to grind my teeth and yell a lot, but the whiskey might help at that."

"For God's sake, Eldred, don't scream during the operation. Davey and I are pretty damn frazzled already. Your carrying on could put us over the edge."

"If he does yell, I'll drown him out with loud praying."

"Maybe God's own thunder will outdo both of you." Seth turned to Kinkaid. "Davey, please give the flask to Eldred and then set him against the wall."

Kinkaid pulled the flask out of his pocket, opened it and gulped down a mouthful. "Iffen you don't mind, I need this about as much as Spenser, maybe more."

"Just so your hand is steady," Seth said.

The boy went to Spenser, gave him the flask and then dragged him under his arms to the wall, where he propped him up. Spenser drank slowly, but steadily. "Not bad stuff. After I drain this flask, you men can take off the leg and anything else and I won't care one damned bit. I'll amend that remark. Please leave my sex apparatus alone. I'm sure I'll figure out a way to make love to a woman even if she has to mount me." Kinkaid took the bedding outside.

"Maybe if you're a really good—and quiet—patient, we'll have a woman waiting for you after the operation." Seth looked around the

108

room. "Damn. Davey, we've got a problem. That storm has darkened the room and we may not be able to see too well. Then, we may make a mistake and cut off Eldred's testicles instead of his leg. Seriously, we have to have more light at the table."

Kinkaid started looking through drawers for extra candles, first in the cupboard and then in the chest. He found a half dozen unused ones and three that were partially burned. "Will these do? We already have two gas lamps and two large candles in holders."

"I guess they'll have to. But we have to rig all the candles so we benefit from the light but they don't get in our way. Anyone have an idea?"

Jenkins responded first. "Just a suggestion. Suppose you turn around those chairs so their backs are closest to the table. Then, light a candle and drop hot wax along the tops of the chairs. You can stick the other candles in the hot wax and that may be enough to hold them up. What do you think?"

"It sounds crazy, but it may work," Seth replied. The two gas lamps we can place on the little table and bring that up to the foot of the big table, close to where we'll be working."

"What about the stuff you'll need?" Kinkaid asked. "You know, the knife, saw, packing and all."

"I think there'll be enough room on that little table for the lamps and what we need. Speaking of all that, get some scissors for Horace, will you, so he can cut up the muslin."

"I don't know what you folks would do without me," Kinkaid said. "You're mighty lucky— all of you—that I ain't wounded. It seems I got to do everything."

"You're the one who's lucky, Davey, to have come out of this battle unharmed. Be thankful."

"Yeh, Sarge. Okay, okay. I'm thankful," the boy grumbled unthankfully. He found the scissors and handed them and the muslin to Jenkins.

"Eldred, how are you doing?" Seth, who was still seated and storing up energy, looked toward Spenser. He could see that the flask was now nearly empty and Spenser's head was sagging toward his chest. Seth thought he heard snoring. "For God's sake, how will we get him to the table if he's out cold. I never thought about that."

"We'll get this here blanket under him and drag him over to the table and lift him up. How else?"

"You're right, I guess, Davey. I'm just afraid that all that exertion will make me too weak to do what else I have to do."

"You're just going to hafta exert. You don't expect Possum here to rise up and lend a hand, do you?"

"Okay, smart mouth. Don't worry about me carrying my load. Speaking of sharing, let's decide now who's going to do what at the table."

"I already told you I'm not up to operatin', for bein' no surgeon."

"And I'm telling you that part of your exertion is going to have to be working closely with me. Not just watching. You can't be a goddamned spectator." Seth looked toward the couch. "Sorry, Horace." He turned back to stare at Davey's downcast eyes. "How about me applying the tourniquet, cutting away flesh and muscle with my knife and tying up arteries. You do the sawing of bone because that's the toughest part, I think, for me. We can work together somehow with the packing." Kinkaid made no response. "All right, Davey? Did you hear me?"

"I heard you. I'll do what I can, but you're askin' a lot of me."

"Eldred is asking a lot from both of us. I pray to God we can come through for him." Seth stood up and took several deep breaths that only served to remind him of how much his chest hurt. "Okay, let's get Eldred on the table and then we'll set up the candles and everything else. Are you almost ready with the muslin squares, Horace?"

"Yes, and I have the Bible out for reading and praying."

CHAPTER EIGHT
Patient and Doctors

Lightning flooded the room as Seth and Kinkaid made their way to the loudly snoring Spenser sitting slumped against the wall. Seth was without his chair-cane. Kinkaid carried the blanket.

The thunder growled and roused Spenser so that his bleary, boozy eyes met those of the crouching Kinkaid trying to slide the blanket under his feet and legs. "Watcha doin', boy?" he slurred.

"Gettin' you ready to slide over to the table."

Spenser's eyes wandered, unfocused. "Seth, are you there, comrade?"

"Yes, Eldred. It's time. You're as drunk as you're going to get, and we're as skilled and steady as we're going to get."

"Off then, damned leg." He paused and snorted. "Shakespeare, ya know."

"Who?" Kinkaid was not acquainted with the bard.

"From the…er…a…Mac…Shakesperses 'beth play. Doncha know anything, boy?"

Kinkaid gently slid Spenser down from his sitting position against the wall and Seth, kneeling, pulled the blanket under him until the patient was lying flat on the floor on the blanket.

Spenser giggled like any bar stool inebriate. "Damned spot, ackshully, not leg. Get it?"

"Get what?"

"You don't really want to know, Davey. And stop encouraging Eldred to talk. I want him out if possible. Okay, let's slide him to the table."

Seth held the blanket corners by Spenser's head and Kinkaid held the corners by his feet, and jerkily rather than as smoothly as they would have preferred, they dragged Spenser across the floor toward the opposite end of the room and the kitchen table. Soon after starting out they had to fold back the parlor carpet to avoid any additional friction. In doing so, they briefly covered the bottom half of Possum lying with his head to the front of the house.

When they reached the table, Seth dropped his end of the blanket and sat down on one of the chairs that had been turned backwards in preparation for lining up candles. "I have to rest a minute or two, Davey." Although Davey had had the hardest part, still the effort had caused Seth to breathe heavily and painfully. "I wonder sometimes," he said out loud to no one in particular, "whether I'm working on one lung. Sure feels so."

"Now what?" Kinkaid looked at Seth as Spenser lay on the floor alternately snoring and giggling, evidently still in response to his MacBeth play on words.

"What? Oh God, Davey, we have to get him on the table, don't we? I don't know that I'm strong enough."

"Helluva time to decide that."

"I know. I'm sorry, but I get so damned exhausted so quickly. I'm sorry. Let me think. Give me a minute."

"We don't have much time, Seth. He ain't goin' to stay drunk forever."

"May I make a suggestion?" Jenkins had been watching the preparations while cutting up the muslin.

"Go ahead, Horace."

"Get a board about as long and wide as Spenser. Slant it against the foot of the table. Maybe Davey could then grab Spenser by the shoulders and drag him up on the board, with you at the foot of the board to prevent Spenser from sliding down. When you have him in position on the board, both of you can lift up the foot end until the board is level with the table. Then, you or Davey can pull and shove Spenser onto the table."

"What do you think, Davey?"

"I ain't sure that's going to work."

"Let's try it. It sounds easier than me trying to lift a dead weight directly from the floor to the table. Did you notice any loose boards outside on your several trips?"

"Don't recall."

"Please go take a fast look."

"Hey, it's thundrin' and lightnin' out there."

"After what you've been through here the last couple of days, you're worried now about being struck by lightning?"

Kinkaid stomped to the front door and opened it. The rain was coming down hard. "Shit, I ain't no goddamned slave," he muttered as he stepped off the porch.

In less than five minutes Davey was back, rain water dripping off his head and his clothes thoroughly soaked. But he had a board about six feet long and two feet wide. "Will this do? I ripped it off the floor in the summer kitchen."

"Let's see. Prop it up against the foot of the table here."

Kinkaid placed the board at an angle and he and Seth slid the blanket on which Spenser lay so that his head was at the foot of the board. Kinkaid bent down, grabbed Spenser under the armpits and, with a loud grunt, started to drag him up the sloping board until his head was at the top of the board where it met the table. Seth leaned over to hold Spenser's feet to the board.

"Okay, Davey, help me lift the board." Kinkaid joined Seth to lift the board so that it and Spenser were level with the table top. "I'll hold on here if you can slide Eldred off onto the table. Easy does it, now."

"Amazing, it worked!" Jenkins was the first to acknowledge the successful carrying out of his idea.

"Now we have to work fast, Davey. Let's move over the small table and put the candles on the chairs."

Seth had previously placed the saw, his knife, the belt and thread on the small table along with the two gas lamps. He and Kinkaid now placed it at the foot of the table on which Spenser lay. Jenkins gave

Kinkaid the muslin squares and Kinkaid placed those on the small table and put the bucket of water to the side.

"Davey, you light a candle and drip wax on the chair tops and I'll come along after you sticking the other candles into the wax." The two men went from chair to chair, four in all. Out of the twelve candles placed, three to a chair, only two fell down, and Davey managed to put them back.

"Are we ready?" Seth looked around nervously. Kinkaid nodded and Jenkins bowed his head in silent prayer. "Light the candles, Davey, and we'll get started."

"Good luck." Possum, lying on the carpet from which he had not moved since being felled by Zinger, raised his head.

"Thank you, Possum. We sure need it. And if you're religious like Jenkins here, you could say a prayer, too. I'm real sorry we can't do anything for you."

The candles were lit and Seth and Kinkaid stood on either side of the table looking down into the wound in Spenser's leg. Neither one had seen it close up before. It was worse than they had imagined. Whatever had sliced into the leg below the knee—shrapnel or a splinter off a boulder— had gone deep and just to the side of the bone. There was pus in the wound and the skin around it was a horrid greenish-yellow color. The color had begun to spread from the wound toward the knee.

"I think we can still save the knee, Davey. Let's cut just below it. Davey?" Kinkaid had turned away with his hand to his mouth. "Are you all right?"

"I warned you. I ain't got the stomach for this stuff."

"For God's sake, Davey, stay with me. Don't fail us now. I'm going to cut with the knife to the bone and around the bone, and then you're going to have to use the saw. But first, let me tie this belt around the upper leg to cut off the blood." Seth took the belt off the table and tied it around Spenser's thigh. "Oh shit, we need something to tighten the belt as necessary. Davey, quick grab a spoon or something out of the cupboard we can use to twist the belt." Davey brought back an eight-inch wooden spoon. Seth inserted it into the knotted belt.

Lightning blazed through the windows of the little house and illuminated the five soldiers' faces.

Seth's one eye twitched nervously; both eyes showed more strain and fatigue than fear. Panic had taken over Kinkaid's face. His eyes bulged and his nostrils flared. Heavy perspiration now dripped where once there had been rain water.

Possum's hairless, pimply face was hard to read. Mostly what was written there was resignation. The child warrior was resigned to his own unpromising future and, though he had been honest in wishing the team luck, he was resigned to Spenser's dying on the table or shortly thereafter. Jenkins had his eyes closed; he mouthed sacred words that no one else in the room could hear, but the hint of a smile revealed that he was absolutely sure his words were being heard where it counted.

The lines on the face of the soon-to-be amputee moved in all directions. One moment they spread into a grin, the next screwed into a frown, and then gathered together as if Spenser was forming a question or perhaps an exclamation that remained unuttered.

Thunder rumbled across the Emmitsburg Road and down Warfield Ridge like a thousand horse-drawn caissons, then faded into the tall trees and glacial crags on the big round top.

Seth shuddered. "Davey, please hold one of those lamps up here by the wound, and use that spoon to make a couple of turns in the belt." Kinkaid did as he was asked and Seth picked up his knife.

Most men who lived in the small towns and on the farms of Orange County, New York and a majority of counties north and south still hunted game, usually for food but also for sport. In any case, they were not unaccustomed to skinning animals and cutting their bodies into steaks and roasts, stitching their pelts into winter clothing, or displaying heads and hides on the walls of private homes and public taprooms. And not a few men and women had performed some minor surgery on family and friends when a doctor was too far away or too busy, or when one could not be afforded.

So it was that when Seth picked up his knife and began to open Spenser's leg to expose the shin bone, he was neither shocked nor surprised by what he saw. And he knew enough to realize that the toughest part of the amputation, other than to control bleeding, was to cut through the heavy muscle that made up most of the leg.

While Seth was cutting to the shin bone, Kinkaid held the lamp and twisted the tourniquet, but he kept his eyes averted from the surgery. Now, Seth turned to him. "Davey, it's your turn. The shin bone has to be sawed through and I have to sit down somewhere to rest. My lungs are about ready either to explode or collapse. I think I'll bring over that upholstered chair Spenser used to sit in. I'm sure from that position I can still hold a lamp for you and keep a hand on the tourniquet. So far, there hasn't been much bleeding, but we haven't got to the main arteries and veins."

"God, Seth, oh God! You're really going to make me do that?"

"Davey, I told you early on that I just can't do it all. I'm wounded too, you know, and I don't have much strength—much endurance."

"All right, all right, but—oh God."

"He's looking over your shoulder, son." Jenkins glanced over and smiled.

"Uh-huh. Okay, Seth, go get your chair."

Seth, who really was worn down, limped to the upholstered chair and dragged it slowly to the table at Kinkaid's side between two backwards kitchen chairs. As promised, he held up the one lamp and took hold of the spoon stuck in the knot of the belt. "I'm ready."

Kinkaid picked up the saw, swished it in the tub of water and wiped it on his shirt sleeve. "Here goes."

"Easy strokes, Davey. Remember, this is a man's leg, not a tree limb."

"I know, I know. Don't give me a lot of orders, for God's sake."

"Just trying to be helpful. That's all."

The sawing began. Kinkaid's face flushed and paled almost in time with the back and forth of the blade. Seth looked up at him and noticed that his eyes were almost everywhere except on the shin bone and the saw. Sometimes he stared straight ahead, and at other times he glanced out a window at the storm.

"Davey, for Pete's sake, watch what you're doing."

"I am, I am. Shut up, will ya. I'm doin' my best."

"I know you are. Sorry."

Possum tried to avoid the sound of the saw blade grinding through bone by sticking fingers into his ears, and suddenly Jenkins' private prayers became public—and loud. "Lord, guide this young man's hand. Bless Seth and Davey, your instruments of mercy and healing here on earth—in this very room. And we pray that you will save Eldred and allow him to regain his health and vigor so he may attain the full and happy life you have foreordained. Thanks be to you, oh merciful Lord."

"Seth, Seth, for God's sake, I think I'm almost clear through the bone. Now what?"

"Go cautiously. Be very careful now. There may be blood vessels near the bone."

"How near?"

"I don't know. I don't know. But the main artery has to be somewhere close by, I suspect."

"Well, do something. I don't want blood spurtin' all over me."

"I have the tourniquet pretty tight now, Davey. You won't get splattered." Seth stood up. "Let me in there with my knife. I should be able to sever the bone with the knife if you're as close to being through as you say. We'll be less likely to butcher the artery with a knife blade than a saw blade. The saw really could tear up blood vessels and nerves and such."

Seth took his knife from the table, wiped it off with a piece of muslin and bent over Spenser's leg. "Hold that light real close please." Kinkaid, who had taken over the lamp and tourniquet, obliged. Seth began ever so slowly and gently to finally separate the shin bone. It was done. "Now Davey, it gets a little tricky."

"Whaddaya mean tricky?"

"I'm going to have to tie off blood vessels pretty soon and I've never done that before."

"Hell, we've never done any of this here before, have we? I know I ain't."

"You're right. We've never amputated a man's lower leg. It's a first." Simultaneously, they added, "and last time." Seth soaked some of the muslin squares in water and laid them on the operating table at Spenser's

117

feet. Then he gathered up some of the heavy duty thread he had taken from the basket and previously cut into various lengths and laid them across Spenser's good, trousered leg. "Tighten that tourniquet one good notch, will you. Sweet Jesus, there it is!"

"What?"

"The main artery. I'm sure of it. Here goes." He ran his finger across the blade of his knife to make sure it was still sharp. He wanted only clean cuts. "Oh my, oh my, how nice, how very nice."

"What, what?"

"If you kept your eyes open, Davey, you could see what I'm doing. The artery is severed and only minimal bleeding." He took the wet muslin and soaked up what blood there was. "Now, if I remember how to tie a decent knot, I'm going to close off that artery." He took a length of thread and slipped it around the blood vessel. "There. Not bad, if I do say so. But keep the tourniquet tight. There's bound to be more arteries and veins around."

Seth stood up and wiped his face with his sleeves. His hands were shaking slightly and his one eye still twitched. "Let's have a look at our patient. He's been mercifully quiet."

Spenser was pale and breathing deeply and rapidly. He was making noises, but nothing that made sense. Seth put his hand to his forehead. It was cold and clammy. "He doesn't look or feel so good. I think we better finish this operation as soon as we can. That whiskey's going to be wearing off soon."

"At least he's not screamin' or whinin', Seth."

"Yes, that's in his and especially our favor."

"You don't look so well yourself, Seth."

"Far as I can tell, it's only Horace's prayers that are holding me up. When I'm concentrating on the work, I'm okay. When I stop, like now, I begin to feel the pain and the awful tiredness. But we've got to keep going now for Eldred's sake." He returned to the operation, cutting now into tough muscle, occasionally finding smaller blood vessels and then the major vein, all of which he tied off. The difficulty and strain of tying off the small vessels took its toll on him, and his wheezing could be heard even by Horace and Possum.

Horace had taken to singing hymns, perhaps having tired of repeating essentially the same prayer over and over again. He launched into the first line of William Cowper's "There is a balm in Gilead, to make the wounded whole; there is a balm in Gilead, to heal the sin-sick soul."

The lightning and thunder had trailed off to the east, but the rain had not let up. While several hours of daylight remained, the low, angry clouds darkened the room and the flickering candles affixed to the chairs cast strange shadows on the walls. Seth periodically stood straight, arched his aching back, stretched his arms up and out and shook them to relieve the terrible tension. When he did this, his silhouette nearly filled the back wall behind the table. It resembled a gigantic black bird ready to swoop down on the helpless patient.

"Davey, another bone. Not as big as the shin bone. And after that? Well, we're just about done. Will you please take over?" Seth held the lamp and kept his hand on the spoon in the knot of the belt, but he was exhausted. Now, for no particular reason, except perhaps because the operation was almost over, he began to cry. Not out loud. No sobbing. But the tear drops ran down his cheeks and mixed with salty sweat.

"Are you going to finish off this bone like the other one?"

"Yes, I suppose." For the last time, he swished his knife in the bucket and began cutting. Finally, he pulled the ugly, poisoned portion of the leg away. "It's over Davey, it's over. We did what we set out to do." The man and youth shook hands. There was no back slapping, no joyous celebration. The man was near collapse and the youth began to shake all over as though a great chill had snuck up and overtaken him.

"My congratulations to you both." Jenkins applauded softly and briefly.

"Do you think he'll live?" Possum asked.

"I certainly hope so, my boy. I certainly hope so." Seth had two final chores. He wet more muslin squares in preparation for packing the bloody stump. Then, slowly, he released the tourniquet. He held his breath. Had he tied off the arteries securely? Would the thread hold? The bleeding was only slight, so he placed the wet muslin. Lastly, he took two pieces of dry muslin and wrapped them around the packing, securing them with some of the remaining thread. He thought to himself that perhaps tomorrow he or Kinkaid would look for pins that could be used to keep the wrapping on.

"Davey, would you please clean off the table a little, empty the bucket and blow out the candles. I barely have enough air in my lungs to take the next breath."

"I guess." Kinkaid moved in slow motion, as though there were great weights on his feet and hands. "What about this?" He pointed to the cut off leg still oozing on the table.

"Oh God, yes. We've got to get rid of that. I think there are a couple of muslin squares left. Wrap it in them and we'll bury it tomorrow."

Seth pulled the upholstered chair up to the table by Spenser's head and leaned over. Spenser was breathing more normally, and a little color had seeped back into his face. Seth sat there until it was almost dark, slave to a cycle whereby he alternately stared at Spenser in search of a sign and dozed off with his chin on his chest. Kinkaid had curled up on the carpet and was fast asleep.

Spenser was snoring loudly, but no one awoke but Seth. He slid his chair toward the foot of the table where the blanket which had served to drag Spenser to the table still lay in a heap. He picked it up, painfully stood up and draped the blanket over his comrade.

"Sorry, Eldred. You didn't wake up in time for me to take you out on the porch to smell the rain."

Seth snapped his fingers and a brightness flickered ever so slightly in his half-closed eyes. He moved like a sleepwalker to the front door and opened it wide. He turned back toward Spenser.

"Here, my friend, the fresh breeze comes to you. Good night."

CHAPTER NINE
Comrades

After he opened the door, Seth shuffled to his mattress and collapsed upon it. His chest hurt more now than it had on the battlefield. However, the pain was no match for exhaustion and he was asleep before he had a chance even to arrange his body and limbs in an attempt to make himself comfortable.

The storm had failed to drive away the July humidity and it dripped from trees, clung to the grass, and promoted rotting of those blue and gray soldiers' corpses that still lay where they were slain. A sodden breeze oozed into the house, but no one cared.

Seth dreamed.

The war was over and the Orange Blossoms—what was left of them—were going home. They crowded on the deck of a steamer heading north out of New York City bound for Newburgh. The time was either late spring, before the summer heat flattened the Hudson River into shiny glass, or early fall, before the north wind streaked down from the Adirondacks and set aflame the trees standing tall along the Palisades.

The silent men in brand new Union blue lined the portside rail as the ship glided past familiar landmarks.

Past Haverstraw, where at the nearby home of William Smith, Benedict Arnold sold out his new nation to British spy John Andre.

Past Stony Point, where Mad Anthony Wayne's 1,350 soldiers and Seth had clawed their way to the top.

Past West Point, high on a bluff overlooking a double bend in the river, where cadet Pierre G. T. Beauregard paid close attention to artillery instructor Robert Anderson years before Confederate General Beauregard ordered the bombardment of Fort Sumter commanded by Major Robert Anderson.

Seth's dream shifted to the pier in Newburgh, where the steamer docked and the people shouted, "Three cheers for our brave boys!"; the band played a spirited version of "When Johnny Comes Marching Home," and whiskered politicians and community leaders in tall hats smiled broadly and silently praised God for allowing them to remain at home for the duration.

The old soldiers—there were no more young men, the war had seen to that—disembarked and formed ranks. Seth, for no reason explained by the dream, had been chosen to carry the regimental flag, its tatters witness to the crucibles through which it and the regiment had passed.

At a command that sounded afar off, the Orange Blossoms stepped out smartly to begin their parade up Broadway into the afternoon sun and, later in the day, into the embrace of loved ones. Pretty young ladies ran up to give a bouquet and occasionally plant a kiss on a grateful cheek. Little boys threw streamers and old men and women cried, "Thanks, boys."

Suddenly, the bright faces along the wide thoroughfare turned ashen, and from their lips issued a great gasp as though the air had rushed all at once from a giant balloon.

Seth glanced back over his left shoulder to see what terrible thing had happened in the ranks to cause this horrific reaction. Every man, row upon row upon row, was minus his left leg below the knee and the regiment swayed grotesquely from side to side in an awful rhythm designed to keep the men's balance as they marched silent and sullen. "Where are your legs, men?" Seth screamed. "For God's sake, put on your legs for the people."

"Seth, Seth." Kinkaid was tapping him on the shoulder. "I think Spenser is conscious and moaning."

It was dark, but Seth had no idea what time it was. He wiped the precious little sleep from his eyes and the dream from his brain. "Have you talked to him?"

"No, I woke up and heard this noise coming from the table and came to get you."

"Thanks." He didn't mean it, of course. "Help me up, will you. I'm just about out of strength."

Kinkaid grabbed Seth by both hands and pulled him slowly to his feet, where he wobbled for a couple of seconds.

"Let me put my hand on your shoulder and you can walk me over to the table." The two men—soiled, rumpled and soggy—moved slowly toward the table where Spenser's form could be only dimly seen in the blackness of the night. While Seth and Kinkaid had extinguished the candles and lamps after the operation, they had left the chairs turned backward, and the small table that held the surgical paraphernalia was still in place.

"Eldred, are you awake?" Seth turned one of the chairs around and sat down near Spenser's head.

"Yes, I'm still here in the house on the battlefield, aren't I? Not in some purgatory?"

"This house is your purgatory, Eldred, and ours, too. Are you hurting pretty bad?"

"Yes." He was speaking through gritted teeth. "Tell me the operation went well and that I'm not suffering this pain for no good reason."

"You don't remember anything?" Kinkaid asked.

"No, not really. That was damn powerful whiskey you gave me. Say, what did you do with the thing—the piece you cut off?"

"We'll give it a proper burial in the morning," replied Seth, "unless, of course, you want to keep it as a souvenir."

"God, no. But you got it all, the bad part I mean?"

"Yes." Seth pointed Kinkaid in the direction of the little table. "Please fetch one of those lamps and light it will you, Davey?" The youth lit the lamp and brought it to Seth. "I want to have a look at our handiwork."

He undid the string that held the muslin sheet over the wet packing in the stump. He gently pulled the packing off. The wound had been leaking blood and serum, but not profusely.

"I'm going to soak some more muslin and repack the stump," Seth said, "and then I think we'll pin up what's left of your pants leg to cover the packing. While I prepare the packing, Davey, will you hunt up some safety pins? Try that basket down by the fireplace." Seth stood up slowly and painfully walked to the little table, using the chairs to steady himself. He picked up several of the remaining muslin squares, soaked them in the bucket of water they had used earlier, and returned to where Spenser lay. Kinkaid came back with a handful of pins. Seth replaced the packing and then, with Kinkaid's help, he pinned up Spenser's pants leg.

"There. Good as"—he caught himself— "as it's going to be."

"What time is it, Seth?"

"I don't know. We started the amputation late afternoon, at the height of the thunderstorm— remember?—you were still conscious then. When we finished, there was still a little light in the sky. But by then, Davey and I were worn out and we laid down and slept. Until you woke us."

"My apologies for breaking into your well-earned slumber."

"Say, there's a clock on the wall, I think, just this side of the fireplace." Seth pointed to a spot to the left of the kitchen fireplace. "Davey, grab the lamp here and take it over to the clock and see what time it is."

"Davey this, Davey that," Kinkaid muttered, but he did as he was asked. "It's a quarter to three."

The men had been speaking softly, but from the sofa came Horace's Midwestern twang. "Eldred, are you all right?"

"Yes, Horace. These butchers didn't kill me after all."

"We said a lot of prayers on your behalf, comrade."

"And I thank you for that. I guess I needed them. God and whiskey: a powerful combination, kind of a one-two punch."

Possum also was awake. Actually, he had been disturbed when Kinkaid, who slept near him on the carpet, got up to rouse Seth. "Maybe that's what I need," he said, "a bottle of whiskey. Then I wouldn't think so much on Pa and Jeremy and..."

"Yourself," Horace interjected. "My southern friend, many a man and boy, not a few as young as you and as old as me, are going to live their life with missing limbs or bodies that don't function the way they used to—the way they're supposed to. And you and they are going to have to make the best of it. So far, you've been making the worst of a very bad situation, a tragic event that never should have happened, but did. Good heavens, lad, this whole war is one endless tragic event."

"If you're tryin' to make me feel better, sir, you ain't. I weren't no enemy when I came into this house, jest someone lookin' for a place to hide. Your man had no reason to shoot me. None."

"We've been all through this," Seth said. "First off, Zinger was not our man in the sense he did what any Union soldier would have done under the circumstances. Zinger was a killer, probably before the war— at least in his heart. The war, which you folks started by the way, simply gave him an excuse and an opportunity that he wouldn't have had as a civilian. At least he wouldn't have got away with murder. If there wasn't any war, and you and he were civilians, Zinger would have gone to prison for what he did."

"As it turned out," Horace said, "he paid with his life."

"Not for shooting me."

"I'm not so sure, Possum. I believe every man, even Zinger, feels guilt, and in some people guilt can eat away at the heart and mind like a moth inside a wool coat over the summer."

"And we didn't start the war, neither. My daddy said you northerners came down and forced us to fight to protect our land and families."

"All right, let's end it there," Seth interrupted. "There's been enough fighting outside this house without carrying it over inside."

"Can I say something?" asked Spenser.

"Not about who started the goddamned war," Seth answered.

"No, I have two simple requests. One has to do with a promise of sorts you made to me, Seth, and the other has to do with my pipe. I want to go out on the porch and smell the fresh air and smoke my pipe. How about it?"

"Are you up to it, Eldred?"

"I can tell you that I want to get off this lousy hard table that's making my back sorer than my half leg."

Seth looked at Kinkaid. "What do you say, Davey, can we get this amputee off the operating table and on to some softer surface? I guess we cold haul his mattress and pillow out to the porch."

"I don't care if I have to lie in a puddle. I just want out of here for a while." He smiled, barely visible in the flickering light of the lamp. "Speaking of whiskey, is there any left? I don't want to pass out; I just want some relief from the pain."

"Davey, is the flask still around, and are there a few drops for this thirsty man?"

Davey went to the other end of the room where Spenser had leaned against the wall before the operation. "A couple of swallows I think." He brought the flask and gave it to Seth.

"I'd say more than a couple of swallows. My guess is maybe six or seven if we don't gulp."

"We?"

"Yes. I say two or three for Spenser and one for each of the rest of us, Possum included."

"I have to admit that's fair," Spenser said. Seth gave him the flask and he took his three drafts quickly. Then the bottle was passed around until it was empty. Kinkaid helped Possum sit up so he could have his share.

"Now, my friend, let's see about getting you to the porch. Of course, the air has been coming in at you. I opened the door earlier, but I can sympathize with your wanting to get off the table and get out of the house. Davey, give me a hand."

Together, they moved the chairs and slowly raised up Spenser so that his legs hung over the side. He looked down at the stump. "Looks peculiar, doesn't it? I didn't realize what I'd look like. I've seen other empty sleeves and pants legs, but I confess it's a bit of a shock to see a part of yourself missing." He looked at Seth and Kinkaid and then over to Jenkins. "And before anyone says anything, I remember what you said to poor Possum, and you won't hear any complaining from me."

Kinkaid pulled Spenser's mattress and pillow out the front door and returned to the table. They eased Spenser off and on to his good leg. "Put your hands on our shoulders," Seth said. He did so, and the three walked unsteadily out the front door and onto the porch. "One more favor, Davey. Would you please grab the pillow off my bed and bring it here, along with Eldred's pipe and tobacco pouch."

"Yeh, and then I'm goin' back to sleep."

When Davey returned, he and Seth propped up the two pillows against the house so Spenser could sit up while lying on his mattress.

"You comin' back inside, Seth?" Kinkaid asked.

"No, I think I'll move Zinger's rocker out here and keep Eldred company."

"Ain't you sleepy after what we went through?"

"I'm pretty much awake now, thanks." He took a deep breath and grinned sheepishly. "Davey?"

"I know, one more favor. Bring the rocker out. Right?"

"You read my mind. Many thanks."

Kinkaid dragged out the rocker and Seth fell into it heavily. "Goodnight, Davey. Or should I say good morning." Kinkaid went inside and closed the door behind him.

Spenser filled his pipe and lit it. He sucked in a cloud of fragrant smoke and then parted his lips slightly so that the smoke escaped slowly into the night.

"Seth, I owe you my life. You know there's no way to repay you and Davey…"

"…and Horace. His prayers, remember."

"And Horace. I don't think I would have made it another day, I was feeling that poorly."

"Well, we did do a pretty good job, considering we didn't know much about either anatomy or surgery. However, I'll be interested to hear what a real surgeon thinks when we get you under the care of one."

"How do you feel, Seth, honestly?"

"Not well. I encountered a rebel surgeon on the battlefield and he said I'd live, and of course I have, but something's not right inside my chest. I still hurt every time I breathe and the pain is as bad as ever."

"That's another reason I offer my eternal thanks, because you helped me when you yourself needed help. Still do."

"You would have done the same for me."

"I wonder. This has been a strange interlude in the war, these last couple of days. Six men—well, four men and two boys, although we'll have to count Kinkaid as a man now—none of whom knew each other, from different units and parts of the country thrown together. And all but one wounded or, in Zinger's case, accidentally hurt. You have a truly vicious person; a deeply religious one; a child needlessly crippled for life and, I think, emotionally scarred; you and a youth who have never before accomplished anything together other than making coffee and slicing vegetables for our meals having to perform a major operation on someone you hardly know. Do you see what I mean?"

"Yes and no. I agree that this has been a very different kind of experience. Of course, you are thrown together with strangers when you first join a regiment, but then you have days and weeks and years to form friendships and get to learn about your comrades. All that has been condensed for us. It had to be. But you never answered me whether you would have performed the operation on me if our situations had been reversed."

"I hope I would have. I think I'm the kind of person who would, but one never knows. I will guess that our experience here in this house has been unique."

"How so?"

"I imagine you could have a house or hospital ward full of wounded soldiers who never say boo to each other, maybe because of how badly they're wounded, or just because the mix of personalities doesn't generate anything. Think on it a minute. What really jelled us was Zinger, or, more correctly, our almost universal disgust at all that he was."

"And all that he represented."

"That's it, Seth, and what he may have represented most was the evil in each of us. God help me, maybe I could grow to like the killing, to feel nothing inside when I look across a field or stone wall and fire a minie ball into the face of an American who looks like me and has family and friends waiting for him back home in a town that's pretty much like those in Maine or Michigan or New York."

Spenser relit his pipe. This time, after inhaling deeply, he blew smoke rings that billowed upward until they fell apart into mere wisps among the rafters of the porch roof.

This summer night, actually very early morning of July 5, a Sunday, was pretty much like a summer night anywhere in America. Male crickets rubbed their forewings together feverishly so their chirping would remind female crickets where they were and what they were up to. Fireflies by the thousands darted in the bushes and trees and danced among the hollyhocks and snapdragons in the garden, and how they made their bellies glow was not fully understood by any of the 100,000 men who had disturbed their normal rounds these last few days.

Because he was seated in the rocking chair, Seth could see farther than Spenser, and as he looked northeast through trees blasted by shot and shell toward Devil's Den and the ridge beyond, he could see the flickering campfires of Union bivouacs. Seth could envision fellow Orange Blossoms sitting around those fires. Some still would be talking about the battles fought over the last few days, who had been killed and wounded, and who had performed some heroic or cowardly act. How had he been listed on the rolls at muster yesterday and the day before, he wondered? Did anyone know he was still alive? Did his comrades think he had been captured?

He could picture Michael O'Meara sitting on a flat rock, drinking whiskey that he'd stolen from some officer, probably in another regiment, and spinning more of his Irish fables in a brogue that he embellished for just such occasions. The men of Dutch, English and German stock believed only a third of O'Meara's stories. They felt sure that no people on earth could possibly be so uncomplicated in their emotions as the Irish appeared to be. Openly wistful one moment and merry to the point of being giddy the next.

Josiah Sloat, if he was still alive, might be bragging about all the girls who had been in love with him since he turned fourteen and how he had turned down every one because he was still waiting for the right girl, the one willing to mother the twelve children he planned to sire.

Then the faces and the voices faded from his mind's eye, and he turned to look west toward the Emmitsburg Road and the ridge from which Longstreet's corps had rolled like a butternut tidal wave three days ago. "Eldred, I don't see any campfires in the direction of the Confederate army. Not a one. The eastern ridge—our line—is dotted with them. What do you make of that?"

"Maybe they've gone home—back to Virginia. At least our boys haven't been defeated or forced to retreat. God Almighty, do you think we've actually won a big battle?"

"Wouldn't that be something. If the rebs have skedaddled, maybe some of our men will come looking for us today. Waddaya think?"

"I hope so. Then you and Horace and I—and poor Possum—can get some professional medical attention."

"And food and a bath and clean clothes."

Without buildup or fanfare, the breeze freshened and the overcast parted in places to reveal a moon just bright enough to outline the summer kitchen off to the right and the trees that stood like sentinels along the lane in front of the house. But the moon glow was too faint to enable Seth to tell for certain whether black mounds scattered across the field beyond the trees were boulders that abounded in the area or bodies of the unsung and unclaimed. Seth remembered the night of the second when the thing he thought was a boulder turned out to be a dying Orange Blossom.

"How are you holding up, Eldred?"

"The whiskey is masking the pain for now, thank you."

"You know, you talked before how we were drawn to each other through our hatred of what Zinger seemed to stand for. But you also reminded me that Davey and I really didn't know the man we operated on. You're right of course. The only things I know about you are that you come from Maine and that you spent Independence Days eating roasted corn in a cemetery. Is that about right?"

Spenser laughed. "Well, some would say there isn't much more to me, except that I grew up, admired the sea as often as I could, wrote as much as I could and, then — reluctantly — went to war."

"You're not married, then?"

"No. But engaged. Sort of."

"Sort of?"

"Let me put it this way. She's more engaged than I am. In her letters— and I've sometimes gotten more from her in a week than most of my company get in a month or two—she talks about how much she loves me and how she's looking forward to my homecoming and getting married right away."

"I'm engaged. And not sort of. Lorranah Vandergost is her name. Her family's Dutch, like a lot of people where I come from. I call her Goose.

"Goose?"

" From Vandergost. Gost, goose. See?"

"All right. Anyway, I hope you're happy, because I'm not. Absence does not necessarily make the heart grow fonder; if anything, absence makes the heart grow tepid. Mine at least. I don't think I love Mary Anne now, if I ever did, and I know I don't want to get married. I hate to admit it, Seth, but sometimes I lie awake trying to picture her and I can't."

Seth shifted in the rocking chair. It wasn't very comfortable, and he wondered how Zinger stood it as long as he did. Damn stubbornness, he guessed. "What did you do before the war?"

"I had a little college and got a job working on a newspaper in Bath. Reporter and editor."

"How long did it take you to work your way up from reporter to editor?"

"I didn't work up. I was both things at the same time. Small weeklies like the Tatler – named for a pretty fair journal in merrie olde England — can't afford both a reporter and an editor." Spenser had slid down and he tried, not very successfully, to prop himself up. "How about you and—Orange County, New York, right?"

"Yes. Pretty river country, with the big mountains farther north, and historic country. Many of the men in the regiment have ancestors who fought in the Revolution. In fact, that's how their family got the land they live on today. Veterans of that war each got 200 acres wherever they could find it."

"I wonder if the country'll give us anything after this war?"

"Not land, I guess. Too many of us this time and maybe not enough land—at least on the east coast."

"And what was your work before the war?"

"Dairying. My parents don't own much land themselves, but I worked a lot of the dairy farms in the middle of the county, roughly between Newburgh on the east and Goshen on the west. I know that doesn't mean much to you, but it's good land. Well, good for grazing cows. We have about as many rocks as they seem to have around here, so we're not big on raising crops."

"You speak a whole lot better than most farmers I've known."

"Thanks. Considering we live out in the country, I had pretty good schooling. And I read a lot. I even knew what Shakespeare play you were referring to when, in your inebriated state, you uttered a line from *Macbeth*. Do you remember?"

"No, but I'm not surprised. That play's a favorite of mine." Spenser blew the smoke straight out this time. "So, we're a couple of bookworms disguised as cannon fodder."

"Eldred, I hate to break off our conversation, but I'm about to fall asleep. It wouldn't hurt you to sleep some more, if you're able."

"Can you sleep in that rocking chair?"

"Well, I'm about to find out. It's not very easy on the spine, which probably made Zinger all the more miserable and cranky, but I don't want to go inside and leave you here alone, and I sure as hell don't have the strength to get you up. If I yell for Davey one more time, he'll bust out here with Zinger's revolver and shoot me dead. I don't think I could blame him. It's hard being the one able-bodied man."

"Sweet dreams, then." Spenser repacked his pipe, lit it and blew great clouds of smoke into the musty night. Fortunately, the moon was hidden now and it was too dark for him to see the vultures roosting in the trees waiting for the dawn and breakfast.

Seth closed his eyes and rocked ever so slowly. The conversation with Spenser lingered in his brain, and pictures commenced to parade behind his eyes in three dimensions, as though he were viewing the scenes through a stereopticon.

First up was the schoolroom presided over by Cornelia Blake Keats Emerson Leydecker, who, on the first day of class, wrote that eclectic sobriquet in cursive swirls that nearly covered the chalkboard. Of course, only the first and last names belonged to her. The others were some of her favorite poets of the moment. Goose's older brother, who was her student two years before Seth, told him that Miss Leydecker had inserted Sir Walter Scott, Edgar Allan Poe and Charles Dickens during the last year he had her for a teacher.

Seth, who, like every other boy whose hormones bubbled and coursed through his arteries, fell in love with Miss Leydecker almost at first sight: young and tall, with auburn hair that fell in gentle swells almost to her shoulders on those rare occasions when she pulled on the ribbon that ordinarily knotted those gorgeous locks.

The picture now coming into focus was Miss Leydecker sitting on a stool so close to Seth planted in the front row that he could smell her perfume – lilac, he thought, or some sweet flower whose fragrance melted him like butter on a skillet. She wore no glasses – not like the old,.cold Miss Thorpe before whom he later learned history. The late afternoon sun blazed through the west window to highlight the red in her hair and naturally blush her cheeks. "I'm going to read to you one of my newest, favorite poems." Her voice flowed like syrup. "It is called *Days*, and it was only recently given to us – you and me and all the grateful world – by Mr. Ralph Waldo Emerson of Concord, Massachusetts. "Pay close attention. Think about it on your way home today, dream about it tonight. Tomorrow we will hunt for all the meanings." Her brown eyes searched out the gaze of every student assembled on that late November day more than ten years ago when the maples outside the schoolroom door flamed red, orange and yellow. Then, from memory, with her eyes closed and her countenance radiating the joy that poetry always tendered her, she read aloud:

"Daughters of Time, the Hypocritic Days,
Muffled and dumb like barefoot dervishes,
And marching single in an endless file,
Bring diadems and fagots in their hands.
To each they offer gifts after his will,
Bread, kingdoms, stars, and sky that holds them all.
I, in my pleached garden, watched the pomp,
Forgot my morning wishes, hastily
Took a few herbs and apples, and the Day
Turned and departed silent. I, too late,
Under her solemn fillet saw the scorn."

When she concluded, the room was hushed. Boys and girls who didn't recognize nearly enough individual words to enable them to fully comprehend the poem's meaning were, nevertheless, in awe of its totality as it had poured forth from the lips of the lovely Miss Leydecker.

New picture: The scene was center square in Goshen, the seat of government for Orange County. The time was late spring of 1848. Crocuses had blossomed during a short string of warm days in early March and then shriveled under a mid-March snow storm; they had been followed – as always, and in order – by daffodils, forsythia and tulips. A warmish breeze caressed a crowd of nearly two thousand men, women and children as they stood under a cloudless, friendly sky. Seth, who had just turned eleven, stood next to his father, his hand completely enclosed in the older man's oversized, coarse mitt.

"And now ladies and gentlemen," bellowed a bewhiskered gent in tall hat who even now Seth could not identify, "I am pleased to present to you the sisters Sarah and Angelina Grimke, who have come all the way from Charleston, by way of New York City, to speak to you of the evils of slavery."

As the pictures of that day clicked by, Seth viewed them with the eyes and memory of the child he was then. The sisters were dressed nearly alike; both were richly attired, and their shoulders were covered in fine shawls that protected them from a northern clime they were not yet altogether accustomed to. Each wore identical brightly colored, flowered hats that, to the young Seth, appeared to spread far enough in all directions that they could serve as parasols if called upon to do so.

Almost nothing of their talk remained in Seth's brain, but he still could envision Pastor Breathwaite of the First Methodist Episcopal Church clapping loudly and exclaiming "Amen!" at the end of almost every sentence uttered by one or the other sister. And right after that picture, a tall, gangly man dressed all in black came into view, his black eyes glaring under a black hat. "Go back home and talk to your own people," he growled so loud that he nearly drowned Pastor Breathwaite's amens. "We don't need to hear it." Once, the man turned his dark countenance into the crowd, and Seth was positive he was staring directly at him. Seth pressed himself against his father, who then encircled him with his arm.

No more pictures. Seth fell asleep in that rocking chair on the front porch of that house on that dreadful field of battle two miles south of shattered and shuttered Gettysburg and two states away from Orange County and Goose and fifteen-year-old memories.

CHAPTER TEN
Enemies

Inside the house, Kinkaid was awakened by a noise that, in his groggy state, sounded like just-caught fish flip-flopping in the bottom of the boat. He turned over on his other side and, to his horror, he saw Possum's whole body twitching uncontrollably.

"For God's sake, Possum, what's wrong?"

"I-I-I don't know. I-I-I can't stop it."

Instinctively, Kinkaid threw his body across Possum's lower torso and upper legs. Gradually, the trembling stopped and Kinkaid got off Possum and knelt in front of him on his knees. "There, I think it's over, but you sure as hell scared me."

"I scared myself. I've had this here twitch every so often since I got shot, but it ain't never been bad like this afore."

"I'm goin' to get me some water. Want some?"

"Yeah."

Kinkaid was the only one who had taken off his uniform since arriving at the house. He had stripped down to his underwear and socks before lying down again because his shirt, trousers and shoes were still wet from the rain. He stood up and walked into the kitchen, found in the dark the jug he had filled some time ago and poured two cups. He emptied his in three gulps and walked back with the cup for Possum.

"Here." He raised the rebel so he could drink.

"Thanks, Davey. Hey, that be the first time I called you by name, somethin' other than yank."

"We never really talked to each other before."

"Well, you never seemed too friendly toward me, ya know."

"The same to you, Possum. You made it plain you didn't like yankees. The sergeant was right. You was feelin' awful sorry for yourself. That's for certain."

"Wouldn't you feel bad iffen you couldn't walk or nothin' ever again?"

"I s'pose." Kinkaid was now sitting cross legged next to Possum on the carpet. "Say, what's it like in your army? Did you march hard to get here? We surely did. We was down in Maryland somewhere when we got word to come up on the double. I mean men, 'specially those about the Sarge's age, were droppin' like flies from the heat. We musta lost more'n a dozen before we reached the Pennsy line."

"We came up through Maryland, too, but on the other side of the mountains. We wasn't movin' too fast, neither, 'cept as we got really close to the town. Fact is, we was enjoyin' ourselfs most of the way. We hadn't eaten' so well in months. The pickins is slim in Virginia these days. Some boys, my brother included, slaughtered a couple of beef cattle we came across..."

"Came across? You mean stole, don't you?"

"I wouldn't say stole as much as took. Well, anyways those cattle were butchered and roasted and, oh my, we had fresh vegetables and peaches. I swear I never ate so good, not even back home."

"You just said about your brother and all. When you was unconscious after Zinger knocked you down, we found a letter you'd written home, and in it you talked about your pa and brother. Jeremy? Is that your brother's name? I wonder what happened to them—your pa and brother."

"All three of us was in the same South Carolina regiment—the seventh—but pa had kinfolk in the third, and he was visitin' with them when all mighty hell broke loose with all the cannons firin', first ourn then yourn. Shells was comin' through the tree tops and knockin' down branches right and left. Lord, the man next to me had his skull busted open by a big limb that hit him square on the top of his head. It were awful. Well, we wasn't s'posed to be in the fight that day 'cause we was under Longstreet and had got pretty cut up the day before."

"Don't know about that. We was in that same battle."

"So, me and Jeremy and a bunch of the men was runnin' here and there trying to find some shelter from the cannons, ya know. Weren't much shelter under the trees o'course."

"This here house is pretty far from your lines, ain't it?"

"I'm gettin' to that. Anyways, our boys had filled up some houses closer to our position, so we kept goin' until we could tell we was out of our division and began runnin' into boys from Alabama and Texas. They wasn't gettin' pounded as bad as us, but we was runnin' so hard it was like we couldn't stop."

"Nobody tried to stop you? I know when I lit out, the... Go on."

"Oh, some big Texan—he musta been more'n six feet for sure—cursed at us and jabbed at us with his bayonet, but he missed."

"Then you saw this house?"

"Yeah, runnin' down from the ridge we spotted this place and...Well, you know what happened then."

"But what about Jeremy, your brother?"

"I dunno. I guess I'll never find out about him or pa."

"Do you think Jeremy got to wonderin' whether he might be accused of desertin' if he holed up here and turned around and went back?"

"I never thought about that. I reckon I figured...I s'posed he..."

"Was killed? But no shells were explodin' around here that day. Noisy as all get out, but no bursts over our heads." Kinkaid leaned forward closer to the boy three years younger than himself. "Possum, tell me true. Would you have gone back to your regiment after the shootin'? I mean if you hadn't been shot and we hadn't kept you as a prisoner?"

Possum stared at Kinkaid without blinking. "Course. Wouldn't you?"

Now it was Kinkaid's turn to stare, but he looked blankly toward the window. Then he cast an eye toward the sofa where Jenkins was sleeping. "I'm not so sure," he whispered. Again he looked over at Jenkins. "I ran, too."

"You ran? From what?"

"From the lousy war. From gettin' killed, that's what."

"When did you run?"

"Day before you. On the second. The 140th—that was my unit—Pennsylvania—we were gettin' pushed back not far from some peach orchard. At times it was hand to hand. Say, I recall somebody thinkin' we had Carolinians in front of us. Well, as I was sayin', we were givin' ground— but fightin' somethin' fierce all the way—and a couple boys started to run toward the rear. I followed and I never stopped till I got here, but I don't even remember how I got here. I musta somehow, somewhere passed through your lines and never got stopped or shot or nothin'. It's all a blur now."

"You came through our lines during the battle? That's hard to believe."

"I guess now that I remember it was pretty dark by then and the shootin' was about over and...I got through. That's all I can tell you."

"And you never fired your musket?"

"What made you ask that?"

"I was half awake when the man you call Zinger was cursing you for not firing your gun."

"He called me a coward, the no good bastard, but I ain't no coward."

"Didn't nobody in your company say nothing about you not firing?"

"I guess I fired some."

"But you told Zinger that..."

"Will you shut up about Zinger. I ain't no coward, I tell ya. I don't have to prove nothin' to nobody, 'specially a reb."

"I'm not sayin' you're a coward or anything like that. Some might say I even deserted by runnin' in here. God a'mighty, what they 'spect of you and me?" Kinkaid suddenly fell silent and turned his head away from Possum. "Hey, what's wrong with you? I said I don't put no blame on you. This war ain't so..."

Kinkaid turned back and tears streaked his face. When he spoke, his eyes were downcast and he sniffed back the tears. "I made up that part about not firing my musket. I fired it all right." He paused to wipe his nose and face on his arm. "Smack in the...He weren't more than two feet and...his face kind of..." Kinkaid's body shuddered. "After that I didn't fire no more."

"After what? I didn't catch what you said."

"For God's sake, you need all the lousy details? All right, I'll give 'em to you. I was kneeling behind a rock—one of the thousands in this goddamn place—and had my musket resting on the rock ready to fire. I was sightin' on the reb line fifty or so feet away when all of a sudden this reb—older than us, with a beard and...and this big grin on his face—popped up in front of me. I don't know where the hell he come from, but there he was. Maybe he'd been wounded earlier and was lyin' down t'other side of the boulder. I don't know, but there was his face directly in front of me."

"And you fired?"

"Yes. As I said, I had my finger on the trigger anyways, and he scared me so that I just squeezed and..."

"You hit him?"

"Hit him, hit him? I blew his face and that silly grin all over the rock." Kinkaid's body shook again.

"Why didn't you tell Zinger and the others that story? Why'd you let him call you a coward? You tellin' me the truth now? And why me, anyways?"

"I'm not sure why. Zinger woulda loved me tellin' what I just told you. Hell, he'd like my account of killin' more than he liked his whiskey. Maybe the memory of that reb's face exploding was too fresh—too awful. Or maybe..."

"Maybe you feared the opinion of the others here more than you was afraid of what Zinger thought."

"Could be. I just don't know. And I don't want you blabbin' this to Seth and Eldred. Promise?"

"Sure." Possum put his arms under his head. "Say, Davey, do you figger both of us has been listed as deserters?"

"Oh, God, I hope not. I don't think of myself as a deserter. Besides, I've been caring for the wounded. What's wrong with that?"

"Right, and I was wounded by the enemy, and what's wrong with that?"

"And my heart's about ready to give out, and what's wrong with that?" Jenkins spoke from the sofa. Kinkaid, startled, spun around to see him curled up facing out.

"Sarge, how long you been listening?"

"Long enough. But, boys, I judge neither one of you. We all have our secrets, some worse than others, some that disturb the soul more than others. Take me, for example. I have a bad knee, all right, but I could probably do some walking on it if I had to."

"You mean you coulda helped out with the operation and all?"

"Well, I thought I did help some, but, yes, I could probably have done a little more around here without collapsing because of the leg. But I was afraid."

"'Fraid of what?" Possum asked.

"Afraid that my heart would give out. I'm getting too old for this war and for fellows your age. What with the forced marching, the fighting and the heat, I'm about done in. I've been having a lot of pain across the chest and down my left arm. It seemed to be getting a little worse last night...well, whenever we went to sleep... By the way, do you know what time it is now?"

"Not exactly," Kinkaid replied, "but it must be close to dawn by now. Seth and I moved Spenser out on the porch just before three o'clock. Then I came in here and went to sleep."

"How is it you ain't told nobody about your heart?" asked Possum.

"Oh, mostly pride I guess—vanity the Bible calls it. I wanted you all to think I was stronger than I am, that I could do as much as Davey here if it wasn't for the bayonet wound in the knee. Can you understand what I'm saying?"

"Sure," Kinkaid answered, "you were worried about others' opinions as much as me."

"Boys, let's make a three-way pact. I don't ever mention to anyone what I overheard, and you don't tell anyone what was said here in the dark. It was a time for soul-searching and soul-confessing. It probably has been good for all of us, don't you think?"

Kinkaid spoke first. "I agree to the pact, but I don't feel no better. I was just beginnin' to get that reb's face out of my mind."

"I swear, too, but none of us has really done no wrong."

"All right boys." Jenkins spoke more softly. "I can't see either of you too well in the dark, but that's no matter. Join me in a little prayer, will you?" The youths were silent. "Heavenly father, we've bared our souls a little tonight—or maybe this Sunday morning—and we pray for your forgiveness for anything any of us has done that needs forgiving. Amen."

"Amen."

"Amen."

Jenkins lay back on the sofa and thought of home smack in the middle of lower Michigan, close to the Indiana border. Home was a modest frame house that stood under elms that commenced growing in the last century, and the prairie was flat for much, much farther than the eye could see. No wonder people in the Dark Ages were scared to walk too far lest they fall off the Earth's edge, Jenkins thought; they surely wouldn't have ventured any distance from his house. His knee throbbed, his chest ached every time his heart forced blood through narrowing arteries, and he was soggy with sweat.

He remembered summers when he was first married. He and his wife would hitch their frisky mare Marmalade to a wagon, throw in a tent and as much non-perishable food as they could put together, and head for the eastern shore of Lake Michigan. There, they set up their tent on great, rolling dunes and at night flung wide the flaps and lay exposed in their underclothes to catch the cool breeze that began in Canada, drifted down the lake, and at last eased its fifty-five degrees on shore.

Now, from the deepest chamber of his saved soul came Jenkins' anguished, silent plea, "My God, oh my God, why hast thou forsaken me?"

While all was quiet now in the little house on the southern end of the battlefield, in this hour before the sun rose above the Hudson River and Orange County, arched over Philadelphia and Lancaster County, and before its rays crept up and over the round tops and descended into the fields of death, thousands of men were stirring.

The Federal Fifth Corps, under command of Uncle John Sedgwick, was boiling coffee and preparing to move forward from the protection of cemetery ridge in pursuit of the retreating Army of Northern Virginia.

At the head of Lee's army, slithering like a wounded serpent back to the Potomac, was a wagon train bearing thousands of wounded soldiers. Their moans and shrieks, for the roads were terrible and the men lay mostly untreated and unfed on plain boards, rent the night and caused even the most ardent Union sympathizers along the route to weep in sympathy.

Some men of the Orange Blossoms and of other units were being roused and told that this day they would work as burial parties and would have to beat the vultures to the dozens of rotting corpses that still littered the farms and woods of this portion of gorgeous Adams County.

Across the border in nearby Emmitsburg, Maryland, Jeb Stuart's cavalry was passing through, taking out on the people of that little town their frustration at having failed themselves and Lee at Gettysburg.

Among those persons disturbed by Stuart's raiders were the photographers Alexander Gardner and Timothy O'Sullivan, up from Washington and staying overnight at the Farmers' Inn & Hotel. But they were about to get up anyway, so they could get an early start for Gettysburg, where, they had heard, a great battle had been fought.

"What's Philadelphia like?" Possum asked quietly." I never been to no city, not even Charleston."

"It's big, of course. Probably bigger than some whole county in South Carolina. You do have counties, don't you?"

"I reckon."

"You reckon? You don't know?"

"We don't worry a whole lot about counties one way or t'other. We stick pretty close to home and the river."

"Well, Philadelphia is on a river – the Delaware. Ever heard of it?"

"The river? No."

"Well, it comes between Pennsylvania and New Jersey. Anyhow, Philadelphia sits on the west side of the Delaware and – you've heard of the Declaration of Independence haven't you?"

"Sure. But what I mean is what do you city boys do? I hear tell you work in factories most the day and night, and right along with the niggers you keep tryin' to take away from their owners."

"Me and my folks don't live in the city proper. We have some land, and my father is a wheelwright."

"Are all the men in your regiment city boys? And ain't most of them foreigners?"

"We're a mix. And what do you mean by foreigners?"

"You know, not real Americans. Why, Pa tells of yankees captured in Virginia who couldn't even speak English. Pa said they sounded like they was clearin' their throat and then spittin' out their words. Kinda like squirtin' tobacco juice into a spittoon." Possum laughed at the notion.

"You're probably talkin' about Germans. We got some, but they're Americans all right. Where did your people come from?"

"Huh? My pa and grandpa was born in the same house we live in now."

"Before them, I mean. Did you come from Indians, or what?"

"All I know for sure is our army is all Americans."

"You make me sick, reb. We're American as much as any goddamned rebel. Remember that. And we're not all city boys, as you say. And we aren't stealin' your goddamn blacks. They come to us because you people beat up on them."

Jenkins intervened again. "Boys, we're all Americans."

"Shit."

"Shit."

CHAPTER ELEVEN
Ngugi Wa-Tu Kataama

Dawn was just an hour away from showing itself above scarred and bloody round top as the black man hurried along what once was a plainly marked path down Warfield Ridge from the Emmitsburg Road, but which had been almost obliterated by caissons' gouging wheels, horses' pounding hooves and tramping southern feet, some shod and some not. At his side was a boy about five whom the man's wife had given birth to, but who carried the male chromosomes and genes inherited from his white father and the man's master, Theodoric Laban Castleberry II.

Theodoric Laban Castleberry I owned the better part of Conecuh County in Alabama's rich black belt, where cotton blanketed the land south from Montgomery to the docks at Mobile. The First had given the Second 1,000 acres and 200 slaves for his twenty-first birthday. The Second — called Ted by his mother, sisters and friends, but Theo by his father – managed his property well and impregnated five black women, including the one called Jin, who was married at the time to the man Theodoric labeled Hercules because of his broad shoulders and strong back, but whose hidden and never-forgotten African name was Ngugi Wa-Tu Kataama.

Ted, now twenty-seven, was a lieutenant in the 48th Alabama Regiment in Evander McIvor Law's Brigade, John Bell Hood's Division and James Longstreet's First Army Corps. His unit had struck the Union line on July 2 just to the left of Seth's Orange Blossoms, closer to the Devil's Den. The 48th was among the rear guard of the Army of Northern Virginia, now, on the fifth of July, limping like a wounded bear toward a Potomac crossing, but a bear whose claws could still maul and maim anyone or anything that came after it.

In the half light, Kataama saw ahead the outline of a house, quiet and isolated among the bruised fields, remains of ancient glaciers, and remains of young men. Where there was a house, he naturally assumed, there had to be a well and water. Neither he nor his son, Akono – merely Boy to Theodoric Laban Castleberry II — had had anything to eat or drink since just before dark last night. At around midnight, Kataama had awakened his son where they had bedded down under a wagon to prevent being soaked by the rainstorm.

"Get up very slowly, Akono. Make no sound; don't break even the smallest twig lessen it make a noise in the master's ear." Akono did as instructed, and together father and son left the encampment five miles west of Seminary Ridge, avoided the sentries, and followed the ruts and detritus left by the retreating army.

"I don't see a living soul here 'bouts, Akono. S'pose we take ourselves over to that well yonder and get us a long drink of water if we can and then lay our tired bones down under a tree and wait for Mother Sun. In the light, we can begin lookin' for Father Abraham and his army. What do you say to that?" The child was silent.

Kataama had taken but a dozen steps when the child pulled on his shirt sleeve and pointed toward the porch of the house. He followed the boy's finger and dimly saw the form of a man slouched in a chair on the porch. "Oooh," he sighed, "there be somebody here. Maybe the owner. I won't be disturbin' him right yet, but later, when Mother Sun make herself known, we see if these kindly northern folk will give a free African and his son somethin' to eat."

The pair walked slowly toward the well on the side of the house, but they suddenly froze when they heard and then saw a horse and rider galloping down the ridge. As the horse drew nearer, the rider waved a sword over his head and screamed, "Hercules, you black son-of-a-bitch, stop or I'll cut off you and your boys' testicles and feed them to hogs."

Theodoric Laban Castleberry II had awakened three hours ago and wandered into the woods to pee. As he returned to his tent, he looked around for his manservant and the unwanted result of his irresponsible catting. When he couldn't locate them, he knew they had run off. Hercules had escaped once before, about eleven months ago. That time, the Second had cornered him on the bank of a river at flood tide, brought him back to camp after tying his arms securely to his body, and then beat his bare back with a branch plucked from a willow tree.

This time, he had borrowed – virtually snatched – an artillery horse and rode east. Where else would Hercules and the boy go if it weren't back to the Union lines. He hoped he could catch up to his property before they got too close to Federal pickets; otherwise, he'd risk being captured. No nigger was worth that.

At the sound of the rider's blare, Seth sat up straight, his eyes swept clean of sleep in an instant. Spenser groaned and tried to push himself up, but fell back on his pillows when sharp pain traveled from the stump upward into every other part of his body.

A faint hint of dawn had slipped down off Cemetery Ridge and gathered speed as it illumined first the valley and then Warfield Ridge in its rush toward the Blue Ridge. Seth saw that the rider had reined in his horse next to a man and a boy, who appeared to be black in the gray light. The rider hadn't noticed Seth and Spenser on the porch. He placed the point of his sword on the right shoulder of the man, and even at close range he continued to yell.

"Thought you'd escape did you? Took advantage of the confusion, did you? Well, you aren't going anywhere, except back with me. You belong to me still."

"But master, we was…"

"I don't have time for talk, Hercules. As it is, I've got to catch up to the army. I'm out here in the open alone, do you understand? Even now some yankee bastard could have me in his gun sights. So, you and your boy are going to get on this horse with me, and we're going to go back the way I came—and quickly. Hurry now, climb up here, the boy first and then you. The horse will hold all of us."

"Just a minute there." Seth stood up and walked shakily to the front of the porch and held tightly to the railing. "Who are you and what do you want with these people?" There was enough light now so Seth could see that the rider was a Confederate officer. His uniform was wrinkled and dirty and his stubbled face was smeared with dust and sweat. The rider turned in his saddle to face Seth.

"Who the hell are you? Do you own this place?"

"No, I am a Corporal in the One hundred twenty-fourth New York Regiment and I and several others inside, including one of your men, are wounded."

"You realize, of course, I could take all of you prisoner and march you back to Virginia." The rider, at least so far, had not reached for a revolver and it did not appear that he had a musket, only the sword he still brandished. "But I don't have time to round you up and I suppose none of you is able to walk a long distance anyway, right?"

"Correct. I've been shot through the chest. My friend here on the floor of the porch had his lower leg amputated, and…"

"Yes, yes, I see. Well, I won't bother about you so long as you let me claim what is rightfully mine—this man and his boy, whom my family has paid for and who have served us faithfully since before and during the war. Now, I really have to be going." He turned away from Seth and again addressed the man and his son. "All right, Hercules, help the boy up here. Now!"

"Emancipation." Spenser said the word weakly, but Seth heard him and called to the rider. "Don't you know the President freed the slaves more than a year ago. That man and boy are no longer yours; they are free—free to go anywhere and do whatever they please."

"Yank, if you're talking about my president, Jefferson Davis, I don't recall him doing any such thing. If perchance you are speaking of your president, the one who sits in Washington, I can assure you that no southern gentleman of my acquaintance would pay the slightest attention to anything that tyrant said. Do I make myself clear? Now, for the last time, Hercules, put your boy up here on the horse, or I swear I'll run this sword through both of you."

Kataama grabbed Akono by his shirt collar and the seat of his pants and started to push him up toward the outstretched hands of the rider. Seth wobbled down the stairs off the porch.

"Yank, don't come any closer and don't interfere. I'll cut you down with this sword like a stalk of grain. Move back to the porch." Seth stopped and leaned against the porch for support. He knew he was no match for this reb.

Just then, the front door flew open and Kinkaid stepped out onto the porch. He held Zinger's Colt revolver in his right hand and pointed it at the reb officer. "Mister, we're gettin' sick n' tired of your givin' orders. You're on Pennsylvania soil and we don't own no slaves and don't much care for others ownin' 'em. Now, you can let those people go and be on your way—and I reckon you want to get back right quick to your beaten army—or I'm goin' to put a Union minie ball between your eyes, through your heart or up your ass. You decide where. You ain't got but a few seconds to make up your mind." Kinkaid cocked the revolver.

The rider looked coldly at Kinkaid, muttered something and let the boy's hands slip from his grasp. Kataama caught him and the two of them moved away rapidly in the direction of the porch.

"If I hadn't lost my revolver in battle, yank, I probably could've taken it out of the holster and fired before you could get off a shot."

"Don't be so damned sure. I may be young, but I'm fast—fast enough to outgun a reb officer any day."

"You braggin' little squirt. I have a good mind to…"

"Better listen to him, reb," said Seth. "I've seen this young man shoot down at least a half dozen of your men in a row—and they had guns in their hands, unlike you. Get the hell out of here while you're still sitting pretty on your nice horse. Git!" The Confederate's horse must have thought the command was intended for it because it turned and sped back up the ridge with its rider swearing mightily on this first Sunday in July and waving his sword wildly, but no longer menacingly.

Seth applauded. "By God, Davey, you're a bona fide hero, I swear. Worthy of the medal of honor to be sure."

Kinkaid, trying to hide the quiver in his gun hand and knees, blushed. "I knew I had 'em, but thanks for lyin', Seth, I mean about me shooting the six rebs and all. Truth is, of course, that I never fired a revolver in my life."

"And never a musket, either. I remember what you told Zinger."

"Well, what I told Zinger wasn't entirely true, because…I…when the…oh, forget it; it don't matter none."

Seth turned his attention to the man and his son, who hadn't moved since getting away from the horse and rider. "Hello. You're among friends here. Are you going anywhere in particular or are you just trying to get as far away as you can from your former master and the Confederacy in general?"

"Goin' to see Father Abraham."

"Uh-huh. Well, President Abraham Lincoln lives pretty far from here and you may have some trouble getting in to see him."

"No, I mean to find him with his army — your army." Kataama pointed in the general direction of the Union line.

"Yes, the army is there, but Mr. Lincoln isn't."

Kataama's eyes showed surprise and hurt, and the muscles in his face went slack. "Father Abraham not with his army? Where he be, then?"

"I'll explain that to you, but come up on the porch. I have to sit down." Seth moved back to the rocking chair and fell into it. He had used up most of his energy reserve yesterday and the unrelenting pain in his chest was draining even what little remained. Seth surmised from what the man had said and how he had reacted to his revelation that he believed Lincoln was physically at the head of the Army of the Potomac, perhaps sitting on a giant white stallion just behind the front line and barking orders to his subordinates.

The man and boy came over to the foot of the steps. "We want to hear you, mister, but we is mighty thirsty. Can we go to the well before we come to listen to your story?"

"Of course. It's just around the corner of the house."

"We seen it before. We was headed that way when the young master…" Kataama stopped in mid-sentence and smiled broadly at his son, whose hand he held tightly. "No longer master, praise be to the Lord above."

"You go drink and then come back here." Seth looked up at Kinkaid. "Davey, is there a cup for drinking at the well?"

"Just a bucket. I'll get a cup." He walked inside and brought out a cup, which he handed to Kataama.

Kataama extended his hand to Kinkaid. "Lord bless you, mister, for what you done when master Theo came to fetch us." The two shook hands and then Kataama led his son to the well.

Kinkaid went back into the house, mostly in response to questions being shouted from inside by Jenkins and Possum, who wondered what all the commotion had been about. Seth turned to Spenser, who had said nothing since whispering the word emancipation. His comrade looked pale, his eyes were closed, and thin pain lines showed on his face, particularly at the corners of his eyes and mouth. "Eldred, are you awake?"

"Yes." He opened bloodshot eyes that seemed to have receded into his head.

"I don't have to ask how you're feeling."

"Without the whiskey, I'm not much good, I guess. Do we have any more?"

"No, we finished it last night, or rather early this morning."

"I was afraid of that. Maybe if I could sit up a little better, smoke my pipe and listen to the tales of this black man, I wouldn't hurt so badly—or at least not think about it so much."

"Davey," Seth called to the man for all purposes.

Kinkaid came out. "Possum is kinda upset we didn't ask that reb officer if he knew anything about his pa and brother."

"Unlikely. He wasn't more than a junior officer, so I guess he'd have little knowledge of people outside his own regiment." Seth stroked the four-day-old stubble on his chin. "Unless, of course, he was from Possum's regiment, but...too late now. Can you give Eldred a hand? He wants to be able to sit up a little against the wall."

Kinkaid took Spenser's pillows and puffed them up as best he could. Then he gently grabbed Spenser under his armpits—he was getting pretty good at playing nurse—and dragged him up so his back and head rested on the rearranged pillows. He also found Spenser's pipe and tobacco pouch. After rooting out the ash and partially burned tobacco from the bowl with his penknife, Kinkaid refilled the pipe and gave it to Spenser.

Spenser lit the pipe and, as always, savored the fragrant cloud of smoke. "Davey, I'm going to write a letter to the surgeon-general and recommend you for a promotion to the medical staff."

"How's Horace?" Seth asked.

"Oh, he's fine. Wants the black man and the boy to come see him." Kinkaid leaned toward Seth and cupped a hand over his mouth. "I 'magine he wants to pray over them." The three men chuckled.

"I'd like to talk to the man," Spenser said. "I confess I have never talked to a black man. Never even saw one until I joined up and we went south."

"I think that's true for most of us," Seth said. "Some of the wealthy families in Newburgh have negro servants, and our colonel had a negro servant, but he always kept to himself except when he was helping Colonel Ellis."

"I wonder if they're as bad off in the south as we heard." Kinkaid joined in. "My daddy took us one Sunday afternoon into Philadelphia to hear a...whatchcallit...abo..."

"Abolitionist?" Seth volunteered.

"Yeah, that's it. He preached some kinda sermon. Said the negro slaves were whipped and chained and families were torn apart. Oh my, he was somethin'."

"Maybe this man can tell us how much of that is true," Seth said. "And here he comes."

Kataama and his son came around the corner and sat down on the porch steps. "Lord, Lord, how sweet that water." He looked up at Seth and Kinkaid. "Do y'all have food?"

"Food? God, we haven't thought much about food since yesterday afternoon. I'm not sure what's left. Nothing inside the house, I don't think. How about the summer kitchen or the cellar, Davey?"

"I can make coffee in the summer kitchen and there may be some stale bread left, but the cellar is pretty empty."

"Well, if you don't mind—and I suppose you're past that stage now—maybe you could put together whatever you can. If we ask Horace nicely, perhaps he could turn that stale bread into a couple of fresh loaves."

"With jam, please," Spenser added.

Kinkaid went off to the summer kitchen.

"Who was that officer you worked for?" Seth asked.

"Long, fancy name: Theodoric Laban Castleberry the Second. He be with the 48th Alabama. A lieutenant. Oooh, they got cut up real bad other day. They done lost a powerful lot of men. Master Theo swore somethin' terrible. And cried. Never saw a growed man like him cry so."

"How long were you his slave?"

Kataama ran his hand across his eyes. "I'm tryin' to remember." He looked off into space. "Well, since I wasn't much older than my boy Akono here."

"Your parents were slaves, then?" Spenser asked.

"Oh, yes. Way back. I heard stories of some of my folks comin' to the plantation way before the Castleberrys owned it, when Father Washington was the emperor."

"President," Seth corrected. "George Washington was our first president."

"Uh-huh. That's how long my family be slaves to the white man."

"Did your master beat you a lot?"

"He never 'round that much. But the white man that worked us hard, he sometime hit us."

"Why would he strike you," Seth asked, "just to be mean?"

"Oh, he mean all right, but most times he whip someone for not doin' all he wanted. Didn't carry 'nough, didn't pick 'nough cotton. Sometime when you don't move fast 'nough."

"Did you ever try to run away?"

"Yes, once. Didn't get far, though, and was beat for tryin'. Some got killed escapin'."

"I thought I heard that reb officer call you Hercules," said Seth. "Is that your name?"

"That what old master — Theo's father — call me. Because I was strong, he say. But my African name is Ngugi Wa-tu Kataama."

"What does that mean?"

"My name."

"I know, but what does it mean in English?"

Kataama looked from one white soldier to another, then changed the subject. "Where's Father Abraham's army?"

"Yes, I did promise to explain that," Seth said. He took a painful deep breath. "President Lincoln...let's see...he's like George Washington, the head of all the people—black and white, north and south, east and west. He governs...er...he rules from a house in a big city called Washington—named for George Washington. He says what he wants his armies to do, but other men—generals—command the armies and do what Mr. Lincoln wants done."

"Sometimes," added Spenser. "Sometimes, the generals do what they damn well please and we pay for their mistakes."

"Uh-huh." Kataama listened carefully and his son watched each speaker intently.

"You know what I'm talking about," Seth continued. "The southern armies—like the one you just left—are commanded by generals, too. Lee, Longstreet, men like them. I'm sure you've heard of them."

"Oh yes. I seen the great Lee ride by one day. Everyone raise a shout, ya know."

"So, we can direct you to Mr. Lincoln's army, but you won't find him there. Understand?"

"Uh-huh."

"Is the boy your son?" asked Spenser.

"Yes."

"He hasn't said anything. He just sits next to you and looks scared."

"He be scared. Akono be quiet since the other day when all them cannons went at each other. Boom, boom, boom! The boy, he dove into a ditch and I had the devil time draggin' him out when the noise be over." He looked down into his son's face. "Say somethin' to the man." The boy hid his face in his father's shirt. "See? Nothin'."

Kinkaid returned with half a loaf of bread and a pot of hot coffee. He set them down on the porch and went inside the house to get cups and to see if any of the apple butter they had enjoyed two days ago was left. He found very little, enough for one slice of bread. When he returned to the porch, he offered Spenser the jam.

"God bless you, my boy."

Kinkaid cut the bread into slices with his knife and gave a slice to each person on the porch, including himself. He saved two for Jenkins and Possum, which he took into them along with the coffee pot. Everyone devoured the bread before they touched their coffee.

"A thought," said Spenser. "Suppose Davey were to guide this man – Kataama?— and his son to our lines and then return with a doctor and stretcher bearers—perhaps an ambulance. What do you think?"

"Great idea." They exchanged sheepish grins and Seth called for Kinkaid.

The door opened very slowly and Kinkaid emerged, standing with his feet wide apart and hands on hips. "Now what?"

Seth tried inducement. "Are you still hungry, Davey?"

"Yeah. Why?"

"I know where there is more food."

"All right, where?" He sounded skeptical but interested.

"In our lines, just over there." Seth pointed toward the round tops. "And?"

"We thought you might want to guide Kataama and his son over to our lines and grab a decent meal at the same time." Seth winked at Spenser. "And bring back a doctor and ambulance. What do you say?"

"All right, I guess, but will you men be able to get along without me? You know how you are—always wanting this or that."

"We'll manage," said Spenser, smiling, "but it won't be easy."

"When should I go?"

"As soon as you and Kataama finish your coffee," Seth responded.

Kinkaid squatted next to Kataama. "If you're 'bout ready now, I'll take you to President Lincoln's army."

"Oh, yesiree, I be ready." He stood and raised up his son, still holding his hand. He swept his right arm to take in all on the porch. "Lord, I do love you yankee folk. Bless y'all." He and his son stepped off the porch." He looked at Kinkaid. "Now, mister, lead us to that promised land over there." He pointed east.

Kinkaid got in front of them and together they walked toward the new day.

CHAPTER TWELVE
The Photographers

Jenkins lay on his side, the only position in which he was comfortable now. The bayonet wound in his knee was infected, and the knee had ballooned into a large cabbage; the pain in his chest almost never subsided anymore. Silently, he prayed and groaned and prayed. From his Sunday School memory of learned Bible verses, he brought forth John's revelation of the new Jerusalem and the comforting voice from the holy throne:

See, the home of God is
among mortals.
He will dwell with them;
they will be his peoples,
and God himself will be
with them;
he will wipe every tear from
their eyes.
Death will be no more;
mourning and crying and pain
will be no more,
for the first things have
passed away.

In between a groan and a prayer he heard a noise from the floor where Possum lay. It sounded at first like the thrashing he and Kinkaid had witnessed before. Then, that stopped and he heard heavy breathing. My God, he thought, perhaps the boy is gasping for air.

"Possum, are you all right?" He knew, of course, that he wasn't. There was no answer, and now the sound was almost like a hen clucking, and Jenkins was pretty sure what that meant. He had heard that rattle just before his grandfather succumbed to pneumonia and again after Chancellorsville when a comrade from Michigan who had contracted small pox unexpectedly rolled over on his back and died.

"Davey. Seth. Come quickly!"

It seemed like minutes, but it was only seconds before Seth appeared at the door, leaning against the jamb. "What's wrong?"

"It's the boy, Seth. Dear Lord in Heaven, I think he's dying."

Seth came into the room and bent over Possum. He looked into a child's face. The pimples that once stood out on his cheeks and forehead now blended into the boy's skin as it went from pale pink to white to almost gray. "Possum, can you hear me?"

Silence.

Seth got down on his knees and put his ear to the boy's open mouth. Nothing. Then to his heart. And again, nothing. The eyes that would never again look upon the Salkehatchie River stared dumbly at the ceiling. Gently, Seth closed them. He got up slowly.

"He's gone, Horace."

"Poor boy. Damn Zinger in hell. Damn him."

"He never belonged here, never belonged in uniform. Why do we have to go on killing children? What answers does your Bible offer?"

"None to that question, I'm afraid. This is a holy war, Seth, but…"

"But children are not supposed to get in the way as we die and make Confederates die to make men like Kataama free."

"Seth, you know as well as I do that the other side thinks nothing of putting boys in the front lines."

"We're not much better, Horace. Look at Davey. He's only a boy. And I think something has happened to him that he's buried deep down in his soul – or at least his belly. Hell, we all may be scarred for life in here where it really counts and really hurts." Seth thumped his chest and winced at the discomfort.

"You're right, I'm sure. Poor Davey...." Jenkins's voice trailed off as he recalled the conversation between Kinkaid and Possum he overheard and the pledge each of them made.

"By the way, Horace, you don't look too well." Seth spied the knee bulging with pus that was about to bust loose from the soiled bandage that hardly contained it. "You may be facing amputation, too, but not at my hands I quickly add. Now, we have to decide what to do with Possum. I know I can't drag him outside alone. I've got to think about it — sitting down." Seth sat down heavily in the arm chair Spenser had used.

He sighed a sigh heavy with three days worth of hurts, fears, and resentments; then, he closed his eyes.

Dearest Goose: I want to cry. But the sobs are stuck in my gullet and the tears can't seem to escape from behind my eyes. This is the third day since I was wounded and still no surgeon has looked at the holes in my chest and back. Will we ever be rescued? Does anyone care that Eldred is in pain from an amputation performed by amateurs who may have done more harm than good, and are they aware that another one of their holy warriors is losing his own battle against a rotting knee and a failing heart? And now, Goose, a boy enemy, whom one of our number – the departed and despised Zinger – turned into a victim, has died. What do we do now: drag his lifeless body by the feet bumpity-bump across the floor, out the door and down the porch steps? Will he then become simply another lump on the landscape waiting for whoever or whatever finds the body first – burial party with shovels; buzzards with sharp, tearing beaks; or ground animals with long and bloody incisors? God, I want to talk to you, to see you and touch you. I love you so much and miss you so much.

Dearest Yank: You may not be able to cry out, but I hear your stifled weeping across the miles, and it pains my heart, in part because of your anguish, but also because I am not there to console you, to press your head against my breast and dry your tears with my hair. I, too, long to hear your voice, to spend an afternoon – and for days ever after – talking about a wedding, not war; about a life together, not the death of friends and loved ones; about raising a family, not burying children who stood up to cannon and musket. I close, darling, with a little poem to lift your heart. You know how I like William Blake, and I reread his Laughing Song just the other day. You remember it, I'm sure.It goes like this:

When the green woods laugh with the voice of joy,
And the dimpling stream runs laughing by;
When the air does laugh with our merry wit,
And the grass hill laughs with the noise of it;
When the painted birds laugh in the shade
Where our table with cherries and nuts is spread,
Come live and be merry, and join with me,
To sing the sweet chorus of "Ha, Ha, He!"

When, Seth, you are home with me for good, then indeed we'll sing sweetly to each other. Oh, what a glorious time that will be.

****

As Private David Kinkaid of the 115th Pennsylvania strode tall and straight in front of Kataama and his son, his bearing resembled that of an officer leading his company into battle or on parade. He had tucked the Colt revolver into his belt and his pants bulged at that spot.

Kataama kept pace, his head held high and his big right hand completely enclosing his son's left hand. The boy, from time to time, started to fall behind and his father gently tugged until his son was again at his side.

The big roundtop slightly southeast from the house was Kinkaid's guide, and he led the little troupe to the left of it, heading more eastward. Unknowingly, they retraced almost the same path that Seth had followed to the house on Friday, down the ridge into a wooded valley where the morning's humidity covered the ground in a fine, damp mist. Yesterday's storm had forced the stream that meandered through the hollow over its banks and the trio sloshed through mud that sometimes oozed up as high as the men's ankles.

Kinkaid located a spot where they could cross the stream by stepping on rocks and a fallen tree. Kataama carried his son on his shoulders to ford the stream. "Almost there, boy," he said over and over to reassure the boy and himself. "Almost to the promised land."

"Halt!" A huge man in faded blue uniform, with his sergeant's stripes half ripped off the sleeve of his jacket, popped up from behind a granite outcropping. His musket was pointing at Kinkaid. At his command, two enlisted men emerged from the same hiding place, muskets at the ready, and a third man appeared out of nowhere but must have been hidden behind trees and bushes.

"One hundred fifteenth Pennsylvania," Kinkaid responded smartly. "Bringing in runaways from the rebs."

"Where ya comin' from, soldier?"

"Up the ridge aways." He pointed southwest. "Been holed up in a house with wounded men since two or three days ago. I ain't so sure of time no more."

"Where ya headed?"

"I ain't real sure. I want to turn over this man and boy to somebody that will take care of them, and I'm lookin' for somethin' to eat. And— oh yeah—I gotta direct a doctor and ambulance to the house for the wounded."

"How many wounded?"

"Three of ours and one reb. The reb is paralyzed and the others can't walk neither."

The sergeant lowered his musket. "Mahoney, take this party to Captain Wexhall. Let him decide what to do with them." A skinny private, one of the men who had been behind the granite slab, walked off, waving his hand for the others to follow. He did not speak.

Mahoney's uniform was clean enough so that Kinkaid guessed the young man probably had seen no action but had been attached to a reserve or headquarters unit before being assigned to picket duty—now a safe place to be. The single file slogged through the mud paralleling the stream and then followed its northern branch. When they came out of the woods, Kataama stopped so suddenly that his son, who was slightly behind him with his head down, crashed into his father's rear end. "Ooooh," the old man sighed. "Lord, what a sight."

Mahoney and Kinkaid halted, looked back at Kataama and then ahead to see what marvel had caught his eye. Actually, Kataama's eyes swept back and forth between two marvels.

To their left was a small mountain of granite deposited by an ancient glacier but resembling immense boulders piled high by a mythical giant who strode the land eons before it was called Pennsylvania and before it collected the blood of Americans from such faraway places as Vermont and Alabama.

Along the ridge that stretched north from a nearly barren hill on their right for as far as they could see, thousands of Union troops were assembling rank upon rank. Their muskets were at right shoulder arms; knapsacks, at least those that had not been thrown away during the forced marches of June 30 and July 1, were slung on their backs. Officers, some sitting straight and tall on horses, shouted orders that were passed on by sergeants and corporals.

"It's Father Abraham's army, boy!" Kataama smiled broadly at his son and whacked him hard on the backside.

"Don't tell me there's some kind of grand review," Kinkaid asked Mahoney.

"Naw, they're fixing to go after the reb army."

"Where you taking us?"

"Captain Wexhall is up there just past the roundtop. Com'on."

They walked through the valley between the granite hill and the round top. The signs of a fierce struggle were underfoot and on all sides. Pools of blood and viscera, which were colored neither blue nor gray and wouldn't quite dry because of the rain and humidity, marked where an American died or was badly wounded. Here a canteen roughly gouged by a minie ball; there a pair of shoes from which a gallant soldier, perhaps not entirely sure what his side's cause was, had been blasted out by a screaming shell. The debris of battle was everywhere: a soggy letter from home, a small Bible stained by perspiration, CSA and USA belt buckles so close together that one had to wonder whether on this spot reb or yank had gone at each other with their hands and fingernails.

"It smells." The boy spoke.

"Well now, I hear you mumblin', boy," said his father. "Your voice has come home from wherever you left it." He jerked his arm toward the west. "Yes, there be a mighty smell, boy, but you should be used to it by now. We seen and smelt a powerful lot of dyin' over the last few years." He sighed and rubbed his eyes and nose as if to erase a hundred horrible scenes and bad odors.

"When you're in it—the fightin' I mean," said Kinkaid, "you don't smell nothin'. Most of the time you ain't even aware of all the dying and bleeding around you. I swear—and you probably won't believe me—you hardly hear the noise of the battle. It's kinda like you're all alone. You see what you're aimin' at most of the time, and sometimes you see who's aimin' at you. And not a hell of a lot more." He turned to Mahoney in his uniform unsullied by smoke, blood, urine and feces. "Whadda you think?"

"Sure. Just as you say."

Kinkaid gave Mahoney that look battle veterans—even eighteen-year-olds who sometimes run when about to be overwhelmed and skewered by a bayonet—reserve for those who stand far behind the front line, but later stand on podiums to recount war stories for admiring ladies in broad, flowered hats and brightly-colored dresses.

If Mahoney saw Kinkaid's glare, he gave no indication. "Another thirty or forty yards," he said. "See those tents in the trees. That's where the Captain is."

Captain Verity Griscom Wexhall was a tall man sitting awkwardly on a small stool in a tent that appeared to have leaked rainwater. He wore his whiskers in the fashion of General Burnside and he was smoking a very long cigar. Mahoney and Kinkaid came to attention at the tent's entrance. Kataama and his son stood behind them.

"Yes, Mahoney, what is it?"

165

"Sir, I have a man here from a Pennsylvania unit who has brought with him a black man and child. He wants us—a—someone to take them off his hands."

"Contraband."

"Contra-what?" Kinkaid had not heard the term.

"Contraband. That's what the army calls these runaway slaves."

"Beggin' your pardon, sir, but Spenser—I mean a high ranking Union officer of my acquaintance—told me that President Lincoln had freed the slaves more'n a year ago."

"That's correct, of course. Officially, they are no longer slaves." Wexhall's scowl showed he did not appreciate being corrected. "However, the fact is no one knows what they are anymore or what the hell to do with them. They certainly aren't citizens and definitely not equal to a white man. Even privates." His lip curled as if he wanted to smile but didn't know how to or didn't care to.

"Sir, I have no way to provide for this man and his son. There must be somebody who'll take 'em, and they could use a good meal. So could I if truth be known. I've been takin' care of wounded solders last couple of days and haven't hardly ate nothin'."

"Let me see these contra—these people. Where are they?"

"Right here, sir." Kinkaid pulled away from Mahoney to reveal Kataama and his son.

"You there, what's your story?"

Kataama looked blankly first at Wexhall and then Kinkaid.

"I think he wants to know where you came from," Kinkaid offered.

"From Alabama, general."

"I'm not a general and I mean how did you come to run away. Did you belong to a Confederate officer?"

"I served my master until I see a chance to slip away and find Father Abraham. But I here tell he not here but where Washington lived when he was emperor."

Wexhall directed a frown toward Kinkaid. "Do you have any idea what he's talking about?"

"Yes sir. He thought President Lincoln actually led the army. Into battle I mean. And he's a little confused about presidents and emperors."

"Well, I have more important things to do this morning than trying to figure out the meaning of African gibberish. We're getting ready to move out." He turned to Mahoney. "Take the Africans to brigade headquarters. See the adjutant."

"Beggin' your pardon again, sir, but what about food for the three of us?"

"For God's sake, you make a helluva lot of demands for a goddamned private." He barked at Mahoney. "Take them first to Sergeant Arby. He may have something left from breakfast."

Kinkaid and Mahoney saluted and Kataama bowed slightly, but Wexhall had turned away and was shuffling through orders for the day.

As it turned out, the trio came upon Sergeant Arby at the most opportune moment. At Wexhall's direction, he had earlier set aside for the Captain a sizable portion of good pork—not the fat served up to the soldiers—and freshly baked biscuits. But without the Captain's knowledge he had held out some for himself and was about to dig in when Mahoney brought by Kinkaid, Kataama and his son. Arby tried unsuccessfully to cover the food with his apron, but when Mahoney said it was Wexhall's order to serve these visitors, he divied up what he had, cursing under his breath the whole time. He especially resented sharing his hearty breakfast with a black man. His comrades never ate this well.

The men hardly had time to smack their lips when Mahoney had them on their feet and on their way to brigade headquarters.

Officers and non-coms swirled around brigade headquarters like bees around honey. Some were packing up gear and taking down tents. Others were giving or taking orders, and those that took the orders ran off in many directions to regimental commanders.

Where Wexhall had been tall and skinny, Major Francis Dickerson, adjutant, was short and dumpy. His girth had popped two buttons off his jacket and he was perspiring profusely.

Mahoney interrupted Dickerson's frantic attempts to stuff too many papers into too small a pouch. "Major, sir, with Captain Wexhall's compliments."

"Yes, yes. Speak up. And fast, if you please."

Mahoney obliged and Kinkaid suppressed a laugh as this freshly minted private not much older than himself rattled, "Have a man here who brought in a runaway slave—er—contraband— black man—er— that ran away from his reb master and the private—er—Pennsylvania regiment— can't take care of him and his son—he's taking care of some wounded—and wants us to take the man and his son. Sir." Mahoney took a deep breath.

"Good Lord, man, what will I do with the pair? Can't you see we're going after the damned johnnies." Dickerson looked in turn at the faces of Mahoney, Kinkaid and, finally, Kataama.

Mahoney's Irish mug said I'm fed up with dragging this trio around and please get them off my hands. Kinkaid looked equally exasperated, but his face reflected his desire to get back to the house with a doctor for his friends who, he was sure, depended upon him for their very lives. Surprisingly, Kataama, despite the runaround and callous treatment at the hands of Father Abraham's army, remained elated at being in the promised land at last, and his face showed that and not anger nor hurt, not even the toll taken by years of hard labor and abuse.

"All right, all right. Leave the man and the boy here. I'll place them somewhere. Perhaps some officer needs a servant, or maybe I can place them with a teamster." No one moved. "I said I'd take care of it. Now, get out of here privates and back to your units. You'll be needed up ahead. That's for sure."

Mahoney saluted, turned about and ran back toward his picket detail. It was an awkward moment for Kinkaid. He had never known a black man. How was he supposed to say goodbye to one? He shuffled his feet, scratched his nose and kicked a stone. Meanwhile, Kataama was talking softly to his son. Finally, Kinkaid cleared his throat. "Gotta go." He stuck out his right hand at a startled Kataama, but withdrew it just as quickly and before Kataama had a chance to react.

As Kinkaid walked away, roughly toward where Wexhall and his tent had been, he looked back over his shoulder and saw father and son holding hands, patiently waiting to see what else it meant to be free in the promised land.

Kinkaid became disoriented when he couldn't find Wexhall's

headquarters. He disliked the man, but he thought he might direct him to a field hospital where he could request a doctor, or at least an ambulance.

"What's your unit, son?" An officer on horseback had galloped to Kinkaid's side as he watched dumbly the Army of the Potomac march west in pursuit of the Army of Northern Virginia.

"Pennsylvania. hundred and fifteenth, sir, but I've been away from my unit for several days caring for wounded men in a house beyond the big hill there." He pointed southwest. "They need a doctor. I had to take the leg offen one man and I ain't even a surgeon. But it were my duty."

"Well, I guess that's all right, although God knows we need every able-bodied man in the ranks. A number of people—including most of the medical staff of the army—are staying behind to take care of the wounded, and others remain to bury the dead. I'm sure that if you retrace your steps back to that house you'll come across someone who can help you and your comrades. Good luck." The officer spurred his horse and trailed after Father Abraham's army as it lumbered toward the Blue Ridge like a giant, blue beast of prey.

Kinkaid didn't know whether Mahoney was back on picket duty or had departed with the rest of the army, but he didn't want to chance running into him. So he turned more westward, with the deposit of gigantic boulders and the ridge of which they were a part to his left. Unknown to Kinkaid, the ridge above the glacial remains, what the locals called the Devil's Den, was where Seth's regiment had made its stand.

Each soggy step—the humidity prevented most of yesterday's rain puddles from drying up— took him back in time to the terrible battle of July 2. Of course, he had missed much of it, having left the field when his position was about to be overrun. The merciful God who had attempted to wash away the stains of war with rain seemed to have been no match for the god of war who scattered the paraphernalia of war across the fields like confetti at a political rally.

At one point, Kinkaid tried to walk a straight line without setting foot on a single cartridge or spent bullet. He couldn't go two feet in any direction. Among the litter he found ripped and bloody pieces of clothing—a pants leg, a sleeve, a sock. Occasionally, a pair of smashed spectacles. Even someone's false teeth. He did not come across any dead men, but the bloated, stinking carcasses of mutilated artillery horses still dotted the landscape.

Looking up at the sun, whose heat he felt but which he could not see behind water-laden clouds, Kinkaid guessed it was mid-morning. He also figured he had taken enough of a detour to avoid Mahoney, if he was still in the area, which was doubtful. Why would the army need pickets when the enemy was miles away? He veered toward the southwest in the general direction, he thought, of the house where Seth and the others must be wondering what had happened to him and asking why he had not returned with medical help.

So far, Kinkaid had not seen anyone else, except what may have been a burial party working at some distance north of his position.

Now, as he emerged from woods into a clearing, he was startled to see two small covered wagons and their teams of horses standing unattended. At first, he thought the wagons might belong to burial parties working nearby but out of sight. However, as he walked around one of the wagons, he was less sure of that assumption. This did not look like an army wagon, he thought, nor did it much resemble a carriage a family might own. He started to part the heavy canvas flaps that covered the rear end of the wagon so he could discover what was inside.

"Hey you, get the hell out of there." Kinkaid looked around. The voice belonged to a man of average height, dressed in civilian clothes and sporting a wide-brimmed slouch hat and a scraggly beard. "If you open those flaps you might ruin our pictures."

"Your pictures?"

"Yes. We're taking pictures just aways down the hill."

"Pictures of what?"

"Confederate soldiers, I think."

"You think? The rebs are long gone, mister."

"Not these rebs. They're dead. And putrifying, I might add."

"You take pictures of the dead?"

"Hey, isn't that the result of battles? That's what war's all about, soldier boy—killing. But you know that. Did you fight here?"

"Yes, I fought here, and I guess I killed a few rebs." Kinkaid paused for three or four heartbeats, enough time to imagine that southern face popping up from behind a boulder directly in front of his primed musket like a turkey craning his neck above the protection of tall grass to see whether that last call came from a female in heat or a clever hunter. "One reb for sure."

The man offered his hand. "Percy McPherson. I work for the Misters Gardner and O'Sullivan. I have to bring them a couple more wet plates. Hold on." The young man climbed up on a rung at the rear of the wagon, then threw back a flap and disappeared inside in one rapid motion. From inside he repeated his plea to Kinkaid to stay put. "Give me a few minutes, please."

Kinkaid didn't move. On the one hand, he felt the tug of his obvious duty—to return to the house as soon as possible with a doctor or stretcher bearers or ambulance. On the other hand, he was fascinated by the prospect of photographers taking pictures of bodies on a battlefield. The only photograph he had ever seen was of his uncle—an important businessman in Philadelphia, or so his mama boasted—and his aunt sitting straight and grumpy-looking in their parlor.

McPherson shot out of the back of the wagon carrying two plates. "Com'on whoeveryouare, I gotta get these plates to the photographers before they dry out, although I don't know how anything could dry out in this weather." McPherson ran down the hill, with Kinkaid at his heels.

Kinkaid had seen bodies before, but he was nevertheless struck by the scene at the foot of the hill. Two men stood behind cameras on tripods at different locations and in front of them were five or so rows of corpses. Kinkaid guessed maybe thirty to forty in all. The rows were not all together. The largest concentration of bodies, perhaps fifteen, was the farthest down the hill and the dead were arranged in two rows that formed a V. One of the cameras was placed at the open end of the V pointing toward the junction.

The other camera, closest to where Kinkaid stood with his mouth open and his eyes bulging, was aimed down a line of six or seven bodies.

McPherson handed out the wet plates to the photographers who quickly ducked under their camera covers. No one said anything. After exposing the plates, the photographers yelled for McPherson who grabbed them and rushed back up the hill to the other wagon. Without speaking to each other and completely ignoring Kinkaid, the photographers picked up their cameras and tripods and relocated them. The one taking pictures of the V-shaped formation set up his equipment at the closed end of the V, looking up the hill.

The other man, carrying camera and tripod over his shoulder, called out. "If you're going to photograph from there, I better get myself out of the way; otherwise, I'll be in the picture." He walked off until his colleague yelled, "That's far enough. I don't have you in my sights."

The photographer planning another picture of the V formation fussed with his equipment and waited for McPherson to return with another wet plate. The second man set up his tripod and then sat down on the grass. He took out a pipe, filled it and lit up.

Kinkaid, feeling as though he had intruded onto a private viewing in a very public and wide open place, nevertheless walked over to the row of dead Confederates closest to him. He got no further than the first corpse. The body was lying face down, puffed up grotesquely by the gas of decomposition. When the corpse had been dragged from wherever it had been found in the woods, the man's trousers had been pulled down to reveal his chalk-white buttocks.

"Comin' through." McPherson ran past the transfixed Kinkaid with a wet plate for the photographer who was going to take a picture of the V formation from another angle. He came back up the slope with another plate in his hand. He addressed the photographer resting on the grass. "Aren't you taking anything?"

"Not now. I'd be in the way of Mister Gardner."

"Oh shit, then I have to run this plate back to the wagon, but I don't think it can wait until you're ready. Oh shit." McPherson scampered back up the hill.

Kinkaid walked slowly into the woods and leaned against a tree. He had never seen bodies like this—Union or Confederate. Sure, he had seen men killed, even in his own company, but there was never time to dwell on their dying. And he had never seen a body dead so long that it was beginning to swell and smell.

"Hey, are you all right?" It was McPherson.

"No. What the hell are you men doing?"

"I told you. Taking pictures."

"But a man's behind? I don't care if he's Union or Reb, people don't need to see that."

"People want to see bodies. Believe me. Since these pictures might show up in the north and these here are Confederates, well, so much the better."

"Did you and your friends drag the bodies here? They sure as hell didn't fall down in rows."

"No, no. Apparently, the Confederates had arranged the bodies for burial and then had to skedaddle. It's a real break for us."

"What will you do with these men—these bodies—when you're finished takin' pictures?"

"Nothin'. Somebody'll come along and bury them." Kinkaid started to walk away. "Hey, I never got your name. And you might want to hang around. You never can tell, Misters Gardner and O'Sullivan may want some warm bodies to pose as dead men. Know what I mean?"

Kinkaid did not answer. It was time—long past time—to get back to the house. He muttered to himself, "Please, God, let me find a doctor, or someone who wants to save lives rather than take pictures of the dead."

CHAPTER THIRTEEN
The Stilwells

Elisha Stilwell stood at the kitchen window and watched a red-bellied woodpecker – misnamed, because its head and not its belly is red – shinny down an oak tree backwards. The kitchen belonged to his wife's cousin, Judd Gross, a gruff, bear of a man who swore frequently and attended church hardly ever. Stilwell had never liked him, and now, after spending the last five days with Gross and his tiny, almost invisible wife Gladys in their frame house on the Taneytown Road, he despised him even more. For one thing, the man drank heavily, ate too much dinner too fast, and then spent most of the evening expelling foul-smelling gas wherever he went, which was everywhere, since he was a restless oaf. The woodpecker drilled a snack and then shuffled around the tree out of sight, but the sound of his unique style of dining still echoed in the woods.

Stilwell had to admit that he and his family descended upon the Grosses without warning shortly after noon on June 30. Early in the morning of that day, Stilwell responded to a banging on the front door to their house down from Warfield Ridge. The source of the banging turned out to be a Union captain, who did not identify himself, but announced – and his words still rang like a clarion call in Stilwell's brain, "You had better move your family into town or somewhere east of this area because the reb army is moving in this direction and there could be fighting hereabouts at any time."

CHARLES H. HARRISON

Stilwell closed the door after the captain rode off on a black steed and looked around the room. This house is only eleven years old, he thought, and I and my friends built it stone by ponderous stone – and the outbuildings, too. "It's all going to go; I know it." He muttered to himself while he figured out how he was going to tell his wife, who was upstairs changing the bedding, that they and daughter Lavina would have to pack enough clothes – maybe food – to last them a week or more. One couldn't tell now, of course, where exactly a battle might take place and how long it could last. Maybe – and he was trying to assuage his own anxiety before taking on his wife's – the fighting predicted by the captain will take place north or west of the town and our property will be spared. "No, no, I'm sure it will be in the line of fire and we'll lose everything. Oh God, oh God, be merciful unto us." He quickly added, "And please, while you're at it, have mercy on this house and everything in it."

As it turned out, he didn't have to worry about his wife's reaction to the news or her ability to get belongings together in a short while. She quickly decided they would go to the Grosses, whose house was situated on the Taneytown Road three miles southeast of the big roundtop, and she and Lavina neatly wrapped five days worth of clothes in old blankets and tied the bundles with heavy twine. She also packed one of two stored hams, but reasoned Judd and Gladys "surely can find enough other food to keep us from going hungry. Why, we took them in for weeks when their first house burned down. Remember? They never contributed anything — neither food nor money." She made certain Judd and Gladys remembered as soon as they walked through the front door. "We've come to stay a while because of a battle brewing," she announced on the threshold." It's like when you came to take up residence with us. Remember? Here's a ham."

Today was the second day without the thunderous and terrifying pandemonium that had bounced off the hills, ricocheted back and forth in the woods behind the house and caused Gladys Gross to plug her ears with so much cotton that even now she and Judd were trying to get some unstuck.

The way Stilwell had it figured, he would make the trip to the

176

homestead alone. "God knows what I'll find there," he told his wife, "or what terrible sights I might see along the way."

"Mr. Stilwell"— he and his wife called each other by their Christian names only at the most tender moments they shared, which were infrequent— "I've birthed three children—and almost died twice doing it—saw Uncle Matthew just after he was terrible gored by his favorite bull, and treated the Ferguson twins' horrible burns when they barely escaped the fire that killed their parents. I can stand anything you can."

He had to agree. She was a strong woman, physically as well as emotionally. In fact, as he thought on it, Ermentrude – named for a German grandmother who worked her farm until she was seventy-five — probably would hold up better than he would if they found their house and outbuildings in ruins, which seemed likely considering the events of the last few days.

But he had put his foot down—literally, for he stomped the floor — when sixteen-year-old Lavina quietly suggested she might accompany her parents. "Lord above, daughter, thousands of soldiers remain in the area—hardened by war, far from loved ones. Any one of them could…well, I don't want even to think about it. Mrs. Stilwell, please tell your daughter she must stay here until it is safe to leave. Besides, Lavina, we may have to come back here if our home is badly damaged or destroyed." He nearly choked on the last sentence.

Lavina was their youngest child. Their one son, Joshua, was nineteen and a soldier in an Ohio regiment serving in the west with General Sherman. He had joined up while visiting his grandparents outside Cleveland. The last they had heard from him was a letter informing them that the army was trying to find a way to take Vicksburg on the east bank of the "wide, muddy and finicky" Mississippi River. Another daughter, Rebekkah, was recently married and living in a village above Harrisburg on the west bank of the Susquehanna River..

So it was that at a quarter past ten in the morning of July 5, Elisha and Ermentrude Stilwell set out for home—or what might be left of it. A single horse pulled the wagon. The wagon was necessary, as opposed to a carriage, because Stilwell decided to take back some of the household items they had gathered up hastily when ordered to leave, just in case the place was still habitable. They included a full length mirror that had been in Mrs. Stilwell's family for three generations; two of her favorite quilts; a small, solid oak table that had taken Stilwell three months to finish according to his high standards; and a large, framed landscape by an unknown American artist.

Stilwell also had loaded onto the wagon a quarter cord of firewood, a sack of flour, a bushel basket of peaches and two chickens—all provided by his least favorite relative, cousin Judd.

As the horse plodded north along the Taneytown Road, Stilwell kept one hand on the reins and the other on a loaded shotgun that separated he and Mrs. Stilwell on the seat. He whistled no particular tune in an effort, or so he thought, to keep up his wife's spirits. He turned around once when one of the chickens fluttered its wings and squawked, but he failed to notice the sudden movement under one of his wife's quilts as Lavina quickly drew in a protruding foot.

It was so quiet the Stilwells heard only the clip-clop of the horse's hooves and the occasional screech of a jay or the sweet song of a tanager. The frightening sounds of war that had rattled dishes in every house and caused many a child and adult to hold tight to their seat in the outhouse for fear the thing might be toppled over—those sounds had all been stilled.

Even so, Lavina, sitting in the back of the wagon under her mother's quilt, thought she heard a battle in the distance, because the roar of cannon and the crackle of musketry seemed somehow to be locked in her memory, and the brain had not yet got around to sending a message to the inner ear to turn off the racket.

Almost without a tug from Stilwell, the horse knew to turn west on the road that connected the Taneytown Road with the Emmitsburg Road, which led in turn to the lane where the house stood – or did.

They hadn't gone far up the eastern slope of the ridge that stretched north from the round tops to the Evergreen Cemetery just outside of town when they saw the first signs of the battle— trees whose tops had been lopped off by Confederate artillery.

The road cut across the ridge just below the summit of little roundtop, and the closer they came to that point, the louder grew the din of an army preparing to move out. Above the clamor of shouted commands, grumbling in the ranks, clanging of breakfast pots and pans being stored in wagons, cannons hitched to horses and bugles blowing, one could hardly hear individual conversations of the soldiers lining the road. Occasionally, though, the Stilwells would pass a group of men whose language caused Mrs. Stilwell to cover her ears and the hidden Lavina to pay close attention to words she had never heard before.

"Mornin'," said a tall sergeant with a long scar on his left cheek, "and where you folks headin'?"

"We're going home, thank you," replied Stilwell.

"And where might that be, friend?"

"Oh, southwest of here, off the Emmitsburg Road."

"Well, I 'spect you won't find any johnnies left out there—live ones anyhow—but keep your eyes open." He waved to them as he turned back to a small group of men he was shaping up for the day's march. This was one of those times when Mrs. Stilwell tried to shut out obscenities and blasphemies.

As the wagon slowly rolled down the gentle western slope of the ridge, the spectacle of the seven Federal corps assembling literally took their breath away. They had left their home and the area, of course, before the fighting and just as units of the Army of the Potomac were arriving piecemeal from Emmitsburg and points south. Not until this moment, then, did the immense size of the contending armies impact on them—and this long blue line disappearing into the faraway morning mist represented only the Union side. Lavina stifled a yelp as she peered from under the quilt.

Straight ahead as far as the eye could see toward open fields and orchards was strewn the debris of battle. The Stilwells looked at each other, their eyes speaking of amazement and dread that they would have to cross that awful sea.

Mrs. Stilwell looked into her lap as the wagon wheels smashed into the mud, a Confederate officer's hat, one whole panel off a caisson that had been blown to smithereens, and a Bible cracked open to the lurid accounts of wars waged against the Moabites and Canaanites by

God's chosen people. Unseen even by Stilwell, who cursed himself for his morbid curiosity, were two severed fingers, one wearing a wedding band, that the wagon ground down. Lavina, after staring bug-eyed at the wreckage, lay curled in her hiding place trying to drown out the battle ringing in her ears by humming softly the old hymn "Nearer my God the Thee."

At last they reached the Emmitsburg Road, and there they saw spread out across the flattened fields in every direction small parties of soldiers and civilians. Some of the soldier groups appeared to be burying bodies, while others and all of the civilians were collecting much of what had been thrown away and blown away. An army wagon and one owned by a local resident were equally laden with muskets, canteens and parts of uniforms. Stilwell wondered who the civilians were, if he knew any of them, and whether they would eventually sell what they had gleaned from the bloody plains to the hundreds or thousands of persons who might someday come to Gettysburg to imagine the tumult and perhaps even honor the dead.

Black vultures strutting like beaked mourners and turkey vultures nodding their blood-red heads formed still other clusters, and Stilwell did not even want to consider what they had found to fight over in the dirt.

It wasn't until they reached the top of the lane leading to their house that the Stilwells spoke, and then almost in whispers, as though they expected the ghosts of those who had perished on this land to be offended by their talking about anything so mundane as the status of their crops and the condition of their buildings. Besides, Stilwell, who had witnessed all the sights while his wife only occasionally peeked and then shook her head in dismay, had been traumatized by the carnage beyond his capacity to comprehend.

"Mrs. Stil...Ermentrude...I...I never dreamed it was this dreadful, that the fighting covered so much ground. And I suspect we didn't see the half of it—the battlefield, I mean."

"It looked to me like some families may have lost their homes—certainly everything else they've worked for over the years. I wonder if they'll be able to replant for the fall and winter."

"It's hard to think of corn and wheat and cattle when the mantle of death hangs over this land like a blanket." He coughed long and loudly as though he had suddenly inhaled that blanket and it had stuck in his throat.

Mrs. Stilwell put her hand on his. "I feel a chill like I was coming down with a fever." She hunched her shoulders to fight off the sensation.

For a minute or two they said nothing more. Then that telepathy that comes to most long-lasting marriages brought to their mind at the same instant their son far away besieging a city they could not picture, because neither of them had been farther from home than Hanover to the east and Chambersburg to the west. Each of them prayed silently to the God they believed in and trusted. But buried deep in their soul and not quite reconciled by their faith was a gnawing doubt that God might not be able to save Joshua any more than he could prevent the grisly deaths of the thousands who must have fallen here.

"It's still standing!" Stilwell had caught sight of their house." Praise God, Mrs. Stilwell, we still have our home." He slapped the horse with the reins and the wagon moved down the lane as fast as that old, tired animal could trot. Lavina threw off the quilt and uttered a cheer that was not heard by her parents above the clatter of the bouncing wagon. Her presence was still unnoticed.

"Glory be, I don't think any of the buildings has been harmed, Mr. Stilwell; I do believe we can sleep in our own beds tonight."

Just as the horse and wagon were about to pull up in front of the house, Stilwell saw out of the corner of his eye three buzzards gnawing at something or someone in a clump of trees. In a rage, he grabbed his shotgun and opened fire. Two of the scavengers flew off, but the other blew apart in a cloud of feathers. "Damn, damn, I hate the sight of those godawful creatures. I know they serve a purpose in God' creation, but I can't stand watching them pick apart a human being. I just can't."

When he heard the shotgun blast, Kinkaid raced out the front door of the house with the Colt revolver cocked and at the ready. Seth, who was inside getting a drink of water and one for Spenser, limped behind Kinkaid onto the porch and leaned against a post. Spenser was still lying on the mattress drifting in and out of consciousness. He suffered more each hour, and the leg above the stump was puffy and sore.

Stilwell whirled in his seat and pointed the shotgun at Kinkaid. It was a momentary standoff that seemed much longer to Seth, who stood petrified, staring wide-eyed first at Stilwell and then at Kinkaid and back to Stilwell.

Mrs. Stilwell grabbed her husband's arm in an iron grip and pushed it and the shotgun down. "For God's sake, Mr. Stilwell, they're Union soldiers. What were you thinking?"

"I wasn't. I was reacting. Lord, woman, my nerves are a jangle something fierce, what with all we've seen coming here." He half smiled at the men on the porch. "Sorry. I didn't know what... Say, who are you and why are you at our house?" He tried not to sound unfriendly or inhospitable, although there was a sharp edge to his question.

"This is your house?" Seth hobbled slowly down the steps and then leaned against the railing.

"Indeed it is," said Mrs. Stilwell. "Are you guarding the property? If so, we're much obliged I'm sure."

"Not exactly, ma'am. We're wounded, at least three of us. This young Pennsylvanian has been tending to us." He looked at Kinkaid. "Sort of."

Stilwell got down from the wagon. "How long have you men been here?"

"Since last week. The second day of the battle."

Stilwell helped his wife down and she walked slowly toward the porch. "Have your wounds been treated? Have you had food?"

Kinkaid responded. "I—well, me and the Corporal here—we cut a man's leg off. We've had some food, but not nearly enough I can tell you."

"I'm afraid we've cleaned out your larder, folks," said Seth. "The ham, bread, fruit and vegetables."

"Don't forget the apple butter." Spenser's eyes were open.

Stilwell had joined his wife. "That man lying there, is he the one whose leg was amputated?"

"Yes," said Seth.

"And he's lying on one of our mattresses, and I suppose..."

Seth interrupted. "I'm really sorry, but I suppose we've made a mess of your bedding, and there may be stains on the kitchen table and some places on the floor."

"Mr. Stilwell, please get me my shawl from the wagon." She was chilled again. "May we go into the house?" She couldn't believe she had put the question.

"Of course." Seth was as embarrassed answering as Mrs. Stilwell had felt awkward asking.

As Stilwell approached the wagon to fetch his wife's shawl, Lavina rose up slowly. Startled, Stilwell went for his shotgun.

"Papa, papa, it's me!"

"What on earth are you doing here, daughter? I told you to stay to your cousin's. This is no place for one so young." It didn't occur to Stilwell that many of the boys in blue and gray who had bled into his and other farmers' acres were not much older than Lavina, and some were younger. "Mrs. Stilwell," he called to his wife, "I thought we understood each other that Lavina was not to come with us. This is very upsetting."

"I had no more idea that she was in the wagon than you did, Mr. Stilwell." She turned toward the girl, who was climbing down to the ground. "When I think of the sights we've seen...and now this." She waved her arm toward the house. "I don't know what we'll find inside, and these men are..." She caught herself before describing the soldiers' filthy attire and their odor, which she had detected almost from the moment she left the wagon.

"I'm all right, Mama."

"Well, we can't send her home now, husband. But you stay here with your father while I go inside."

"Hold on woman. I better go with you."

"You're not planning on leaving our daughter out here alone are you?"

"I...I guess not. All right, then, we'll all go inside." Stilwell looked from Seth to Kinkaid. "Will one of you accompany us?"

"Yes. Of course." Seth hobbled up the stairs and led the way into the house. Jenkins sat on the edge of the sofa holding his swollen knee.

"This is Sergeant Jenkins. From Michigan. By the way, the man on the mattress outside is Private Spenser, late of Maine, and the young man with the revolver is Private Kinkaid from somewhere near Philadelphia. I'm Seth Adams. One hundred twenty-fourth New York Volunteers."

The Stilwells glanced hesitantly around the room. Mrs. Stilwell couldn't help saying what all three thought. "It's not as bad as I expected." She read the faces of Seth and Jenkins. Their eyes were downcast and their lips formed a pout. Little boys expecting to be scolded for wrongdoing. "I mean, you haven't disturbed very much. Thank you."

"Ma'am, we were as careful as we could be. We knew we were in the house of good, God-fearing folks." Jenkins the diplomat, Seth thought.

"Aren't you men supposed to get back to your units," Stilwell asked, "and get your wounds tended to?"

"Yes sir," Seth answered. "We're waiting for ambulances now." He shot a glance at Kinkaid that reminded the youth that he was supposed to have brought back medical help instead of a long tale about seeing photographers taking pictures of rebel dead.

For a moment, all stood silent in the middle of the parlor. Then Stilwell spoke. "We were kind of planning to stay now that we're back." He waved toward the wagon outside. "And we have some things to bring in. A table, a painting and such."

"I'll give you a hand, mister." Kinkaid started for the door. "I do all the chores around here. The others are helpless, you know." It was obvious to everyone, including Lavina, that his boasting was to impress her more than anyone. She smiled.

"Do you want a drink of something?"

"I sure could use a drink."

Lavina found a cup and the bucket. "Is this water fresh?"

"Probably not." Kinkaid was at her side before the words were out of her mouth. "I'll refill it." He grabbed the bucket from her and raced out the door, finally laying aside the revolver on the kitchen table.

Neither Seth nor Jenkins mentioned the recently departed: Zinger and Possum. When Kinkaid returned from delivering Kataama and his son, he and Seth, wheezing with each exertion, carried and dragged the lifeless Possum outside. The body didn't weigh more than 100 pounds. Rebels were thin to begin with this late in the war, the CSA having nearly run out of everything needed to nourish a fighting man, and the Stilwell larder hadn't produced enough to add fat where it was needed. Once outside, Seth and Kinkaid laid the corpse in the herb garden next to the summer kitchen, and Kinkaid shoveled enough dirt over it so that all that showed was a shoeless left foot at one end and a shock of straw hair at the other. Seth guessed that burial parties would eventually find the body.

Kinkaid returned with fresh water, poured some into a cup and handed it to Lavina. He expected a sweet thank you and a sweeter smile. He got both and returned the latter.

"Well, young man, you said you'd help us bring things in." Mrs. Stilwell reminded Kinkaid of the offer he'd made to impress Lavina.

"All right, all right." He followed the Stilwells out the door. Seth returned to the rocker on the porch. Jenkins propped himself on the sofa and opened the Stilwell's family Bible to his favorite Psalms.

Lavina ran up the stairs, but soon reappeared with a porcelain doll. She sat at the dining table caressing the doll, even kissing it full on the lips. It had been several years since she had played with the doll her mother had dressed in Sunday-best, including a flowered bonnet with a bow that tucked under the chin. Lavina fondled and hugged the doll now because somewhere between the Grosses' house on Taneytown Road and home, as the family wagon rolled through that bitter wasteland still dotted with mouldering corpses where she and her sister had once gathered wild flowers before the July 4 parade in town, she seemed to have lost three or four years maturity and was again a girl in need of comfort from a close and cherished friend — the doll she called Betsey.

Kinkaid returned to the house with the mirror under one arm and the painting under the other. He leaned them against the wall and then sat down across from Lavina at the dining table.

"That your doll?"

"Yes. Been mine for six years."

"Nice. What do you do around here?"

"I'm not sure what you mean?"

"Well, we go — went — to the city pretty often, but there doesn't appear to be nothin' around here."

"We don't miss going to the city. We've got dances and horse races, grand church socials – lots of things.

"Uh, huh. Whaddya think of the battle. Something fierce, heh?"

"Yes, something fierce." Lavina remembered the sights and smells during the morning's travel and momentarily stared off into space as fresh mental pictures of bloated, mangled horses and smashed cannon blotted out recalled pictures of town picnics on the campus of Pennsylvania College just north of town and acres upon acres of apple blossoms filling the air with perfume on either side of the road to Biglerville.

"I was in the thick of it, you know. The fighting, I mean. Lucky to be alive. I could tell you about standing in blood up nearly to my ankles and...."

"Why don't you tell me about home, instead – where you're from."

Kinkaid was deflated. I can't be a hero to her talkin' about goin' to school and working part-time in a general store, he thought. But he decided to make the best of it. "I nearly swam across the Delaware River once, right where Washington and his army crossed." He hoped Lavina would not ask him to elaborate because "nearly" was less than fifty feet.

"Well, that is something. What's your home like – the house where you live? And your family?" She wondered if he had a girlfriend.

"Oh, like most houses, I guess. I shared a bedroom with my younger brother. He kinda looked up to me. I learned to read early like, and I'd read stories to him almost every night. I was nearly the best student in my school." Again, "nearly" did not bear close examination. He stood nine out of twenty-one. "How are you in school?"

"All right, I guess. I'm sure I'm nowhere near as bright as you from what you say." She ranked thirteen out of fifteen.

Jenkins, who had been reading from the Bible when Kinkaid first came in, now leaned back against the sofa and pretended to be asleep. Actually, the pounding pain in his knee and the ache that ebbed and flowed in his chest had kept him awake most of the night. His face showed a slight smile, but a closer look would reveal how a twinge of sadness had slightly drooped the corners of his mouth. The smile because, in this third year of war, young people could still talk of picnics, apple blossoms, and swimming. The twinge of sadness because it was the third year of war and this boy and girl were both victims.

Mr. and Mrs. Stilwell entered, he awkwardly carrying the oak table and a basket of peaches and she carrying bundles of soiled clothes and the sack of flour. "We could use some help," Mrs. Stilwell said in the direction of their daughter and the soldier who had offered his assistance.

"I've not yet unloaded the firewood," Stilwell said. "Perhaps you – Kinkaid is it? – could start stacking the wood by the summer kitchen. Lavina, you could help your mother by cleaning up the house some."

The youths exchanged glances and smiles and then went to their tasks.

"Horace, I think our saviors approach." Seth yelled from the porch. Jenkins kissed the Stilwell's Bible in his lap and sat up straight on the sofa.

Two Army ambulances slowly descended the lane from Emmitsburg Road. The exhausted horses forced one leg in front of another strictly out of habit and obedience learned long ago. Seth and Kinkaid waved to the driver who didn't wave back. Spenser tried to sit up, but fell back. He was as weak now as he had been before the operation. The men were joined on the porch by the Stilwell family.

The wagons stopped and out of the back of one stepped a man in his forties wearing a long coat that had once been white before it encountered spilled blood and guts and medicines and spattered mud. "Do you have wounded here? We've been making the rounds of the houses on the battlefield. Since early this morning, we and others have picked up some fifty men, both blue and gray. So?" He looked at Seth and Kinkaid.

"Yes," Seth replied. "We have wounded. This man on the floor here had his lower leg amputated. An older man inside has a bad knee and a heart condition. Me...I was shot clean through the chest."

187

"Well, we can take all three of you in the two ambulances. How about you, son?"

"I'm all right," Kinkaid responded. "And I reckon I'll stay here a spell to help this family move back in and clean up a little."

"As you please, but I suggest you check in with your regiment—if it's still here. You may be listed as dead or a prisoner. Even worse, they may've put you down as a deserter. Now wouldn't that be a nasty business."

"I'll look up the regiment as soon as I leave here...a...sir." He assumed the man in the coat was a doctor and officer.

"Bring the litters," the doctor yelled to the two men who were driving the ambulances. They moved as slowly as the horses, but they finally brought two stretchers to the house. "First, take this man here on the floor of the porch. Carefully, now."

The men were practiced at moving broken bodies and they gently laid Spenser on a litter and carried him to one of the ambulances.

"Thank you folks for the use of the house," he said weakly.

The orderlies returned. "Let's take the man inside with the bad knee next," said the doctor.

As Jenkins was carried out, he asked the orderlies to stop on the porch where the Stilwells were standing. "My apology for the mess on the sofa and elsewhere, and a thank you for the hospitality you shared even though you weren't here. Finally, my gratitude for your Bible. It has sustained me these last few days. You will always be in my prayers. God bless you."

The doctor looked at Seth. "Do you need to be carried?"

"No thanks. Davey, will you help me?"

"Sure." Kinkaid took Seth's left arm.

Seth stuck out his right hand toward Stilwell, who grabbed it with both of his hands. "Sir...I don't think we ever got your name."

"Stilwell."

"Well, Mr. and Mrs. Stilwell and daughter, we are grateful for the loan of your home. It was a safe haven at a time and in a place when it was not safe to be anywhere else. Thank you."

"You're welcome," Stilwell replied.

Seth saluted the family and then Kinkaid led him to the ambulance. The doctor joined one of the orderlies on the seat of his ambulance. The horses dragged the two wagons in a circle and headed back up the lane. Seth, sitting in the rear of the one vehicle, waved and Kinkaid waved back.

Dearest Goose: Alleluia! At last we will receive medical care, and — I have not dared to say this to myself let alone speak of it to you – I likely will come home after I've been treated. Perhaps for good. I'm not sure about that last part – staying home, I mean, but some other men from the unit who were badly wounded or suffered from pneumonia or dysentery – and survived – went home and didn't rejoin our ranks. If my days as a soldier are over, dear, then perhaps we can be married before the year is out. I truly hope so. When that blessed day arrives, I think my best man will be a private from Maine I became friendly with these last few days. I may have mentioned him before. He was the one whose leg I amputated. I always thought my best man would either be my father or David Kidd, who I've known all my life, but Eldred Spenser – the soldier from Maine – and I formed a bond out of our shared misery that seems especially strong and lasting. I know I'm not explaining this relationship very well; I don't quite understand it myself. Maybe it's this simple: If you are responsible for saving someone's life – and I believe I saved Eldred's – you are forever responsible for that life in some way. It's crazy, but I imagine his life could slip away if I don't help him hold on to it through our friendship.

Dearest Yank: I'm good at waiting. I waited for you to propose, I waited for your letters after Fredericksburg and Chancellorsville, and I'll wait for your homecoming and rejoice when that day arrives. But I know when our wedding will be. Whatever the year – and I hope it will be this one – the month will be October. I've been waiting since I was seven or eight to realize a dream I first dreamed then. The dream has been vivid in my mind all this time: I'm standing in front of the Methodist Church down the hill from Newburgh in Cornwall on Hudson; my husband is at my side – you didn't get to become him in the picture until two years ago – and the sugar maples surrounding the church and up and down both river banks are ablaze and the air smells sweet and musty at the same time. All my family and friends – and, of course, your family and friends, too – are standing around us smiling and applauding, and the warm afternoon sun finds holes in the umbrella of gaudy foliage and bathes the scene as though its rays were filtered through colored gauze or stained glass. What a grand day that will be, Seth. Now, I can hardly wait for your homecoming.

As the ambulance reached the road, the clouds that had been thickening all morning began to leak, and the drops hit the canvas of the ambulances in a pattern and rhythm that put to sleep Spenser and Jenkins. But Seth continued to watch the house until he could see it no longer.

"All right, we have a house to put to rights," Mrs. Stilwell reminded those remaining on the porch. She and her husband and daughter went inside.

"I'll be there shortly," said Kinkaid. "I have just one thing to attend to out here." On one of his trips outside, he had placed the bundle containing Spenser's severed lower leg high on a shelf in the barn. He ran to it now and lugged it out to the woods, hidden from curious eyes in the house by the intervening summer kitchen. He scooped out a shallow ditch and placed the bundle in it.

He kicked dirt and leaves over the hole and then stood looking at the spot.

He muttered to himself, "After those people scrub down everything, no one will remember we was ever here."

EPILOGUE

Seth guessed it was ninety degrees inside the railroad car, even with fans going at either end. God only knows how hot it must be in those tents that dot the fields of the third day's battle at Gettysburg.

They must be expecting tens of thousands of us from the looks of the encampment, he thought. He wondered how many survivors of the battle fifty years ago would die during this long, hot week of commemoration and celebration.

Seth sold his farm ten years ago when, at age sixty-six, he could no longer give it the care it deserved. Since then, he had lived on the proceeds from the sale and his government pension. His beloved Goose, whom he married on a rainy October Saturday in 1864, died four years ago. She willed to him what was left of her parents' estate. They had no children.

In the same railroad car, which left Goshen in Orange County, New York early yesterday morning, were seven other veterans of the 124th New York Volunteers—the Orange Blossoms. Some of these men were his best friends; the others he saw only at meetings of the Grand Army of the Republic in Newburgh.

But he had not returned to Gettysburg to be with these comrades. He had come to see Eldred Spenser, retired newspaper editor, and Pennsylvania State Senator David Reynolds Kinkaid. The three men had corresponded infrequently over the years, having obtained each other's address through the G.A.R. Seth received a long letter from

Horace Jenkins three years after the war ended, but five years later the G.A.R. listed him as being deceased.

In his first letter to Seth, Spenser reported that he had finally lost all of his leg. Even before he left Gettysburg in August 1863, the surgeons had had to amputate above the knee. Thereafter, what was left of the leg would periodically become infected and swell up. Finally, in 1874, the leg was cut off at the thigh. Since then, he had been free of disease and pain.

Spenser quipped in his last letter two months ago when the three men were arranging to meet on the occasion of the 50th anniversary of the battle, that no one would be able to tell the difference between him and "that sonofabitch Sickles," who lost a leg on the second day of the battle and was now the only general officer left on either side.

Seth was nervous about meeting Kinkaid. Obviously, it would not be proper to refer to him as Davey now that he was a state senator. When they had been together a half century ago, Seth, who was eight years older and only a corporal at the time, had more or less acted as leader of their little group. Horace, of course, was a sergeant, but he never exercised his rank, except one time talking down Zinger—the late, unlamented sharpshooter.

Now Davey—Senator Kinkaid or Mr. Kinkaid—was superior to both he and Eldred, Seth thought, at least insofar as position in society. He concluded that the best way to handle the matter was to be himself, greet Kinkaid warmly for old time's sake and see what developed.

The train came to a stop and the conductor walked down the aisle shaking each man's hand and assisting any who wobbled on legs that were frail, arthritic and nearly numb from hours of riding. To each man, he said, "God bless you" or a simple "Thank you." Most of the veterans interpreted the latter remark as an expression of gratitude for their part in saving the Union, not for riding the Pennsylvania Railroad.

Seth detrained and was immediately swallowed up in a sea of old faces and bodies. Boy Scouts escorted the veterans to their tents, which were organized by state. New York's tents were at the northern end of the encampment, toward the town.

When he and Percival Tompkins of Cornwall arrived in their tent, they immediately took off their jackets and ties and lay down on their cots. They napped until dinner.

The three men who shared four days at the Stilwell house had not decided in advance exactly how they would meet at the reunion. Seth and Eldred supposed that Davey—being younger and having "pull"—would find a way to get them together. One thing they agreed on in their correspondence: They would rent a carriage or an auto and drive to the house. They had to do that much if nothing else.

The next morning, after assembly in the Great Tent, a Boy Scout walked up to Seth. "Sir, are you Seth Adams of the 124th New York Volunteers?"

"I am."

"I have a message for you from Senator Kinkaid of Pennsylvania. You are to meet him at the southeast corner of the Great Tent."

"When."

"I believe he meant now, sir."

"Thank you. By the way, how did you find me?"

"Well, I knew you were part of the New York delegation, and…honestly, sir…you are the thirteenth man I've gone up to." The boy ran off and Seth, who used a cane, walked slowly toward the meeting place.

He was perhaps 100 feet away when he saw an open car standing on the road between the Great Tent and the railroad tracks that had been laid specifically for the occasion. A man was in the back seat of the auto, and a second man stood with one foot on the running board. He waved and Seth waved back. He assumed it must be Davey, but he couldn't tell from that distance.

When Seth was less than fifty feet away, the man standing began to walk forward, a straw hat in his left hand and his big right hand already outstretched. "Seth." It was Davey.

"Senator Kinkaid." Seth grabbed Davey's hand with both of his.

"I believe you have me confused with someone else. My name is Davey Kinkaid, assistant surgeon and general handyman."

Seth laughed. They broke off their handshake and embraced. Both men were teary-eyed. "Who is that stranger in the car. He certainly looks a lot older than we do."

"None of your sass, Adams." Seth leaned into the car and embraced Eldred.

"God, it's good to see you men. Did we—could we have imagined that we would be back here this late in life—on this ground—this hallowed ground?"

"I know I never believed it," said Eldred, calling Seth's attention to his pinned-up pants leg. "I thought this leg—what was a leg—would kill me before the new century."

"Shame on you two," said Davey. "I was always certain we would return here someday, somehow. Even if there hadn't been a reunion. Seth, get in the back seat with Eldred. I'm driving. Next to me on the front seat are sandwiches and cold beer. I even brought umbrellas to keep the sun off you. They're at your feet."

Davey started the car and they drove south until they could cross over the tracks to the Emmitsburg Road. Before long, they were at the top of the lane leading down to the Stilwell house. Trees now hid the house from the road, although they could see the barn. None of them spoke.

Davey turned the car into the lane, and they drove almost as slowly as those ambulance horses had plodded fifty years ago. Then they were in front of the house. It hadn't changed. Not one tiny bit.

Seth and Eldred remained in the car, their eyes fixed on the house, while Davey got out and walked up on the porch and knocked at the door. There was no answer.

"Perhaps they left for the week, what with all these soldiers around," Seth yelled from the car. "Do you remember how Mrs. Stilwell was afraid for her daughter?"

"That family may have moved away from here long ago," said Eldred. "Who knows who lives here now."

Around the corner of the house came a black man in his early sixties. "Can I help you gentlemen?"

Davey spoke to him. "We've returned for the fiftieth anniversary of the battle, and we came here because we stayed here for several days in July of 1863. The men there in the car had been wounded and I took care of them. We thought we'd take a last look at the place for…well, for sentimental reasons."

"Do you work here?" Seth inquired of the man.

"Yes. I also own the farm. Bought it…oh…let's see…twenty or so years ago. And I know you men."

"My God," Eldred exclaimed, "you're the boy who wouldn't talk."

"You found Mr. Lincoln's army."

"Indeed, and I served a Major until the surrender. A true gentleman, he was. After the war, the Major took me to work with him in business in Washington. I was with him 'til he died. All that time I put money aside. One day, I just upped and came back here, with no intention of anything, but just to see what it all looked like around these parts. That's when I found the Stilwells was selling."

"And you bought." Davey leaned against the porch railing.

"Yes sir."

"Do you live here alone?" Seth inquired.

"Yes. It gets kind of lonely. And on summer nights…the ghosts."

"Ghosts?"

"Yes sir. I never see them, but I hear them."

"Do they speak to you?" Eldred asked.

"Oh no, no speaking. Sort of a low moan."

"Wind in the trees probably."

"Maybe you're right, mister, but I'm not so sure."

Davey spoke up. "What is your name? I don't remember."

"Lawrence DeKalb. The Major named me after someone in his family."

"What did your father call you?"

"Akono, my African name."

"Lawrence DeKalb, we have beer and sandwiches in the car. Will you join us?"

"Don't mind if I do."

He and Davey walked to the car. Davey took the sandwiches out of a hamper and plucked four bottles of beer from a tub of ice sitting on the floor. He opened the bottles and passed them around.

"Raise your bottles for a toast gentlemen." They all did. "To the dearly departed, and to the nation that is forever in their debt."

"Here, here."

* * * * *

CPSIA information can be obtained at www.ICGtesting.com
Printed in the USA
LVOW061020171012

303237LV00002B/126/P